Ali

An Inch of Candle

Fontana Lions

WE ARE NOW in the trenches again, and though I feel very sleepy I just have the chance to answer your letter, so I will while I may. It's really my being able to bag an inch of candle that incites me. . . . I must measure my letter by the light.

Isaac Rosenberg to Edward Marsh,
28 March 1918. Before the letter
was postmarked on 2 April,
Rosenberg had been killed.

The author and publisher gratefully acknowledge the author's literary estate and Chatto and Windus Ltd for permission to reproduce the extract from *The Collected Works of Isaac Rosenberg*, edited by Ian Parsons, which appears above.

First published in Great Britain 1980
by Angus and Robertson (UK) Ltd
First published in Fontana Lions 1982
8 Grafton Street, London W1X 3LA
Second impression November 1986

Fontana Lions is an imprint of
Fontana Paperbacks, part of
the Collins Publishing Group

Printed in Great Britain by
William Collins Sons & Co. Ltd, Glasgow

One

DORA TRUDGED UP the hill, pushing Edwin in his perambulator and puffing out clouds into the frosty air. Mother had said, 'Dora, you will *not* be seen pushing the perambulator. Fanny, you will not *let* Miss Dora push the perambulator. Now, out you go, before Edwin starts his noise again.'

But now she half wished she had got Fanny to push Edwin up the hill after all. Her fingers were numb on the handle despite her mitts, and the wheels kept slipping on frozen puddles. Edwin began shouting 'Dora – Dora – Dora!' over and over again until it sounded like a rude word.

They reached the top of the hill. The street in front of them was deserted: not even the telegraph boy with his red bicycle and ominous black despatch case was to be seen. Only a few children were playing on the Green. On the way up the hill they had passed the Lipton's Tea man, and his old horse had left a neat pile of dung steaming outside the church gate.

Dora looked back the way they had come and saw Fanny, way behind, stepping round each patch of ice as if it were a live German.

She said to Edwin, 'Right!'

Then she set off at a gallop. Edwin had half a second to look puzzled, and then he set up a shriek which was half of terror and half of delight as they hurtled down the path, his cries echoing against the elegant terraces on their right, the perambulator bouncing on every stone – and

Edwin, thrown from side to side and up in the air, clutched at his blankets as if he thought they would stop him falling out.

Dora heard Fanny scream 'Miss Dora!' from the top of the hill. She skidded to a stop, not because of Fanny's cry but because she had had a sudden vision of herself with a broken ankle and a bruised face picking up pieces of Edwin from underneath a huge motor car. The perambulator wheels crunched to a halt. Dora panted hotly. She kept her back firmly turned on the approaching Fanny, and Edwin's shrieks dwindled to a plaintive wail.

'Miss *Dora*!' Fanny's face was red and blotchy. She fussed around Edwin, pulled out a hankie to wipe his streaming nose, straightened his blankets, stroked his face. 'Miss Dora, you oughtn't, you really oughtn't – but didn't he love it, the boy, bless him, he really did love it, didn't he? Who's a real boy, full of the rough and tumble? Who's his Fanny's boy? Here, let's have those mitts off so as you can suck that thumb.'

Dora watched the pair of them and thought, now *Fanny* might know. Fanny knew all sorts of things, like how to hitch up your skirts so they wouldn't stop you riding on a toboggan, and what a man looked like when he was having his leg amputated. She knew that Charles Smith, the chemist's assistant, ('Karl Schmidt, see?') was a German spy. She had been to the music hall and knew what kind of bloomers Marie Lloyd wore. What Fanny did not know, to Mrs Fishwick's vexation, was how often to scour Edwin's chamber-pot or how to make mutton hash on Lizzie's morning off. Fanny had been engaged as a pig in a poke, because Mrs Fishwick was desperate. 'Mama,' Dora had written in her diary, 'is on the brink of nervous collapse.' She did not ordinarily call her mother 'mama', but she had been reading Jane Austen and the word seemed to go well with 'brink' and 'nervous collapse'. 'Only a proper replacement for Nannie, she says, will prevent her throwing herself or Edwin into the river. Papa' – here the same literary licence – 'smiles gravely at this, but clearly Steps Must be Taken.'

Steps were taken, and three weeks ago Fanny came to 24 Heathgate. She turned out to be not at all a proper replacement for Nannie. Mrs Fishwick was still desperate. Dora was sorry about this, but to her Fanny was a delight.

'"Edwin is *not* to get out of the perambulator!"' she said, mimicking her mother. Fanny laughed, as Dora knew she would, then removed Edwin's blankets and said, 'Well, boys will be boys, and there's nowt you can do to stop them.'

'Nowt, Fanny?'

Edwin went on hands and knees under the railing and ran joyfully down on to the green.

'Nowt, Miss Dora. I'm not blooming nothing-ing to *you*. Bad enough with your blooming mother.'

Dora laughed. 'Blooming Mother, blooming Father, blooming blooming Richard. Oh blooming war, Germans, Lord Derby and all!'

'Now watch it, Miss Dora, there's no need to blaspheme. . . .'

'That's not blaspheming. Blaspheming's blooming God, blooming Lord Jes. . . .'

Fanny screamed, because at that moment Edwin had tripped over a stone and fallen on his face in the grass.

The sky was a leering yellow. It would snow soon. When the snow was thick on the Green, Dora would beg or steal a toboggan and ride down these slopes, face shining and hair flying. Fanny would show her how. And might Fanny tell her other things, like what made babies? And perhaps even answer that other question for which the words would not formulate in her mind?

The children on the other side of the Green had been playing with a ball. Now they were running away up the slope, over the road and down the alley-way between the terraced houses and the chapel-of-the-strange-sect about which Father had said 'Do not ask such questions'. It was the same when she had been reprimanded for drinking from the public fountain ('To commemorate the relief of Ladysmith, 1900') which stood among the evergreens at the lower end of the Green. 'But why mayn't I?' 'Do not ask such questions, Dora.' Dora had determined to drink again from the fountain, but the next time she and Phoebe went to it they found a dead cat lying over the spout. Thus, she thought bitterly, were her small strivings towards rebellion thwarted.

Edwin was not hurt. After being comforted by Fanny, he got up and ran away, was chased and fell again, was comforted again, and when this had been repeated eight or nine times he got tired. Fanny hauled him back up to the perambulator and settled him in. 'There now. Best be going back home. Look at his rosy cheeks. Who's a tyke, then? He'll be asleep before we're at the church gate, you'll see.'

Now Fanny pushed. Dora asked her about her grandfather and the man with the amputated leg.

'What, again? Bloodthirsty, you are. Well, he lay there, Grandad said. Sweat pouring off him, you could have caught it in a jug. The stink, it was like nothing on earth. All the men, they were throwing up all over the floor. "Got a bottle of whisky?" said the doctor. "Whisky?" said the officer. "I said whisky," said the doctor. "Give it to him. Straight. All of it. This here leg is coming off." Well, at that the man started screaming. . . .'

The first snowflakes fell. The two of them stopped for breath, and Dora held the perambulator while Fanny wiped a drip off the end of her nose with her coat sleeve. The sleeve was shiny with drips old and new. They set off again.

'What did they do with the leg?'

'Well, my grandad took the boot as a souvenir. I expect the rats got the rest of it. See how it's coming down now, a regular snowstorm. He'll be making snowmen in a day or two, and we'll see about that toboggan. Oh, look at him. Didn't I tell you he'd drop off? The lamb. Where's his cover? Look, he's lost his cover!'

'It must have come off by the Green. I'll hold him, Fanny, while you go and get it.'

The snow fell on Dora's shoulders and cold hands while she waited. At first she could watch the flakes separately as they landed on the back of her mitts and rested for a second as if to say 'look at me!' before they melted. Then the flakes fell too quickly to be watched individually, and her mitts were soaked.

'Fanny, you've been ages! I'm like an iceberg!'

'I can't find it, Miss Dora. I've looked and I've looked. We'll have to get him inside somewhere. What shall we do? The poor mite'll be frozen to death!'

'The church?'

Fanny laughed. 'Well, why not the church, miss? I'm sure God wouldn't mind!' The gate creaked, and they went into the graveyard. By some trees on their left was a noticeboard: it was big, painted black with white letters. Dora stopped and read out, ' "Parish Church of St Dunstan-on-the-Hill. Rector: the Rev. Stephen B. . . ." What an extraordinary name! "Bo-san-quet." Do you pronounce the "t" at the end? And look at that!'

To the right of the names of church and rector and churchwarden, obliterating (Dora presumed) the times of services, was a poster. ' "To the Women of Britain," ' read Dora. ' "Some of your menfolk are holding back on your account. Won't you prove your love for your country by persuading them to go? Send a man to join the army TODAY!" '

'Quite right too,' said Fanny smartly.

They hurried on up the gravel path. Edwin shook in his pram, but did not wake up.

'D'you think Master Richard's holding back on your poor mother's account?'

'For *Mother*? Fanny, Master Richard is holding back on Master Richard's account, in my opinion.'

'He's yellow?'

'Yellow as the drawing-room curtains.'

'Not for long he won't be. He's young, he's single, and

he's got to go. Mr Asquith says so.'

When they reached the church door, Dora hesitated. She had never been in a church like this before. 'You go in first, Fanny.'

Fanny opened the heavy door. It swung, stopped, and Fanny pushed the perambulator inside. The wheels seemed to make a dreadful echoing noise on the stone flags. Fanny left Edwin inside and came back to the door and said, 'Come on in, Miss Dora. There aren't cherubim and seraphim in here, you know.'

Dora found they were in a big porch. There were stone-flagged benches along the sides, and she took off her wet mitts, rubbed her hands together and sat down beside Fanny. She started to read in a whisper the names of rectors of the parish since 1342. ' "John de Bohun, 1342 to 1378. Ranulph de Coteville, 1378 to 1380." He didn't last long. "Harold Chadwick, 1830 to 1837. Stephen Haughton Bosanquet, 1898 to blank." Have you ever seen him, Fanny?'

'Yes, I think I saw him once. He looked black – he had a black frock thing on, you know how they do, and a black hat, and his face was all frowning. I was passing the gate when he came out, but he didn't look at me.'

'I've never seen him. A rector – why isn't he a vicar? I didn't even know his name. I've lived here all my life, and I've never even been into the graveyard and seen the noticeboard.'

They sat in silence. They could hear Edwin's snuffly breathing. Dora had left the door a bit open to let in a little light and so that they could see when it stopped snowing. It was snowing more thickly than ever.

' "Or wallow naked in December snow",' said Dora.

'It's the fifth of January. What? Wallow what?'

'Naked. Shakespeare. *Richard II*. "O, who can hold a fire in his hand By thinking on. . . ." Listen!'

Music was coming faintly from inside the church. Dora went swiftly to the inner door and pressed her ear against it. It must be the organ. She hadn't heard music like it before. It sounded regular, full, measured and beautiful, utterly different from the wheezy, whistling organ at chapel.

She sat down and bent over her knees.

'Miss Dora, what are you doing?'

'Unbuttoning my boots.'

'For Lordie's sake. . . .'

She wrenched off a boot and started unbuttoning the other. 'I mustn't disturb the music, must I?'

'You're going *in*?'

The other boot came off. '*Ssh.* Yes. You stay here with Edwin.'

The inner door, miraculously, did not creak. She closed it behind her with scarcely a sound. She walked rhythmically, in time to the music, past shelves of hymn-books on one side and blue hanging curtains on the other, until she was at the back of the centre aisle. Then she stood still and looked around.

It was huge and soaring. The pillars, grey and smooth, seemed to go on for ever until they merged with the roof. The roof was vaulted and intricately criss-crossed, and then the pillars came down, smooth and magnificent, on the other side. The pews all had little doors, and some of the doors had names on. Beyond the pews were some green-carpeted steps, and then more pews, ornately carved and facing each other. On the right of the steps stood a wooden kind of post about as tall as a man, with a carved eagle on top. On the left was what Dora recognized as a pulpit, though it was a great deal fancier than the pulpits she was used to. Then, beyond, was an altar covered in embroidered green, and above it a stained-glass window.

The window was quite the most beautiful thing Dora had ever seen. Figures in blues and reds and yellows stood in columns, with lambs cavorting at their feet and angels flying overhead. Dora supposed they were Jesus and the twelve apostles, but they might have been Moses or Abraham and the prophets. The colours were all that mattered. The strange muted whiteness of the snow falling outside seemed to illuminate the colours and carry them down through the church to where she was standing. The blues and reds and yellows blended with the flowing music, and thrilled her.

She walked slowly up the aisle, feeling as if she were floating. She went towards the sound of the music, and when she reached the top of the aisle she floated up the green-carpeted steps and to the left, towards the carved choir-stalls. Behind the stalls she saw a heavy blue curtain which hid whatever and whoever was behind. Two candles shone inside glass cylinders on big wooden candleholders, and the brass curtain rings twinkled in the candlelight.

Dora looked up and saw above the candles a great array of huge grey pipes: smaller and thinner pipes on the left, getting taller and fatter in the middle, and smaller and thinner again to the right. It was from these pipes that the music was coming. It was so loud now that it made her fingers tingle and her brain freeze. It was not only that she was nearer to it. All those tunes which had sounded so measured and rolling when she had listened to them from the far end of the church now came together like raindrops colliding with each other and crashing down a window-pane. The music seemed to roar like a waterfall and pour over her.

She took a few more steps forward, then turned and stood still. She stared. There, behind the blue curtain, sat a boy of about her own age, playing the organ. He did not see her. He was concentrating totally – as well he might, thought Dora in astonishment. There was not one key-board, but three. Why did he need three keyboards? And all those white knobs on the right and left, what were they? The chapel organ had nothing like that. And look at his feet! He didn't seem to need to get air by pumping al-ternately with his feet on two big pedals. Where did the air come from? Instead of the usual two pedals there seemed to be – yes, it was, a kind of keyboard which he was playing with his feet! She leaned forward. . . .

The boy lifted his hands and feet in the air as if a shell had exploded under him. His face spun round, and he gaped at her. The torrential music was held in the air for a moment, then dissolved away.

'Who are you? What are you doing here?' She saw that he was frightened.

'I'm sorry. . . .'

'Sorry!'

'I didn't mean to give you such a shock. You might have heard me, but the music was so loud, and I took my boots off in the porch.'

He looked down at her feet, and gave a nervous little giggle. He had a soft sort of face, with no spikey features anywhere, and windblown curly hair. He had a large forehead and a chin which didn't quite know whether it was there or not. Dora thought he would be improved by ten more years and a moustache.

His nervousness made her feel confident. 'I liked your playing. I've never seen an organ like this before. Where do you get your air from, and what are all those white knobs?'

'There's a choirboy in the vestry,' he said.

Dora didn't understand, and thought of bats in the belfry, so she giggled rather as he had done. 'What's he doing there?'

'Working the bellows.'

'Oh! Oh, I see.'

'Don't you come to church?'

'Of course not. I go to chapel.'

'Oh, you're one of *those*.'

Dora didn't like his tone, so she asked again, 'What are all those white knobs?'

Instead of replying, he suddenly seemed shy, and turned towards the keyboards. But then he turned back quickly and said, 'What's your name?'

Dora hesitated. Then she said, 'Dora. Dora Fishwick,' and waited for the Defence Of the Realm Act joke or

'*Fishwick?* You mean you're *Fishwick's*?'

Neither came. 'I'm Alfred Bosanquet.'

He doesn't pronounce the 't', she thought. Very Norman. 'The son of the vicar – rector?'

'Rector. A rector is an incumbent whose tithes are not impropriate. A vicar is an incumbent whose tithes *are* impropriate.' He spoke as if reciting dull poetry.

'What's impropriate?'

'I don't know.' He went shy again.

What a funny boy, to know the words but not what they meant. It was almost as bad as Father, who knew what the words meant but wouldn't explain. Dora began to feel rather motherly towards the boy. She was used to young men who were not as clever as her but were bossy, like Richard. But this Alfred Bosanquet must be clever because he could play such a marvellous instrument, and he did not seem at all bossy. 'Please will you tell me about the organ? I can play the piano and sing, and I once tried the chapel organ. But I've never seen anything like this.'

Amazed at her own boldness, she hitched up her coat and skirts, and stepped up and wriggled on to the long bench beside him.

Two

'THE SWEETNESS OF the young girl's innocence,' wrote Dora, who had been reading *Home Chat* for want of anything better, 'released the boy entirely from his shyness. By the time she had to leave, he had confided in her the secrets of his troubled youth. By the time they had known each other a few weeks, her gentle sympathy had persuaded him to throw off his fears and grow at last into a Man.'

She hoped that these final words would prove prophetic, for she was in fact writing on the day after her visit to the church. The truth of the first part was, she felt, beyond dispute. Alfred Bosanquet had not only named for her each manual (not keyboard) and every stop (not knob) and showed her the red-faced boy and his bellows in the vestry. He had also told her, in between examples of fugues and chorale preludes, of his father's bellicose disposition, his mother's nervous complaints, the impossible superiority of his divine (this was Dora's word) brother Humphrey and his own problems with Greek syntax and calluses on his fingers.

Dora sighed blissfully at the memory of her achievement. How had she managed it? Was it the transparent honesty of her face? The sweetness of her smile? (She had only just used 'sweetness'; the number of words suited to *Home Chat*-style prose was very limited.) The liveliness of her mind? Actually, she wondered if he went on about his family problems like that to everyone.

Anyway, she had learnt a great deal of interesting

things about the organ. Eight foot was twice as deep as four foot, and sixteen foot was twice as deep again. Bach's fugues had tunes intertwining like strands of hair in a plait. The swell manual had a special box which enabled you to play louder and softer. There existed organs which had four or even five manuals – he had heard that some in Germany even had six, but of course he didn't dare to ask anyone if it was true. She had learnt a lot of fascinating things, too, about the church. Not all those books at the back were hymn-books. Some of them were books full of prayers, and psalms that were sung to an odd kind of music. Every Sunday morning and every Sunday evening the people who came to church said and sang almost the same thing. 'How boring!' Dora had said. Alfred seemed surprised, and wondered what else you could do. Anyway, the sermons were different every time.

'What are your sermons about?' Dora asked him.

'Oh, mostly about the war. God and our country and all that. He's terribly proud of Humphrey. I feel dreadful, being only sixteen and not old enough to go. I suppose it'll be all over by the time I'm eighteen.'

Dora wondered what he would say if she told him about Richard. Of course she didn't tell him. The less said about Richard the better. Oh, if only she could meet Humphrey! How handsome he must look in his uniform! How his men must adore him! They would surely follow him everywhere and go gladly in his footsteps to their death! Though if they were going to their death, so probably was Humphrey. Banish the thought.

She asked Alfred, 'Wouldn't you be afraid of dying?'

He said quickly, as if pulling out an organ stop, 'Of course not. What could be nobler than dying for England?'

But then his lower lip trembled. 'Some people say there are rats in those trenches, and lice, and bits of men who've been blown to pieces. Father says it isn't true, but. . . .'

Dora said it was probably true of German trenches but it certainly wasn't of British ones, and would he play her that lovely thing that sounded like *O Sacred Head Sore Wounded*?

Dora had been sent immediately up to her room when they got back. Her mother was extremely angry, but mercifully did not ask where they had been. She snatched Edwin out of the pram, horror-struck at his wet blankets and leggings (it had snowed much harder as they walked home than it had done during their sojourn in the church), and despatched Fanny for a clean set before sending her to the kitchen to scrub the table, which she knew Fanny considered beneath her.

Dora, sitting on her bed, flicked through some books in the dim gaslight, but could find nothing which she hadn't read several times already except poetry. None of that took her fancy so she put it back on the shelf.

She stared out of the window. It was almost dark. Snow still fell from a deep slate sky. The light from the lamps in the kitchen shone out in a rectangle over the lawn: Lizzie had forgotten to draw the kitchen curtains again. Mother would scold her for letting out valuable heat, and Lizzie would look martyr-like. Lizzie didn't take much notice of Mother's scoldings. She understood Mother: she knew what it was like to have a babe thrust on you when you had lost all your teeth ('I have *not* lost all my teeth,' Mother had protested, trying not to warm to Lizzie's stolid sympathy, and failing), and Lizzie had rapped Dora over the knuckles once for bursting out, 'Well, why did she have him, then?'

Shrieks and gurgles from Edwin drifted up the stairs. Mother must have had enough of his company and dragged Fanny away from her scrubbing to give him his tea in the nursery. She was probably feeding him the remains of yesterday's tapioca, which he hated. No doubt Fanny would have let him leave it and eat a piece of seed cake instead, but there was no chance of such a transfer while Lizzie stood in the way of the larder.

Dora wondered if she could slip downstairs. She opened

her door a little. The grandfather clock at the corner of the stairs stood at twenty to five. Father and Richard would not be home from the Shop for more than an hour, and Mother would stay in the drawing-room until Edwin's tea was over. Lizzie would be busy with dinner, which by the smell was some kind of smoked fish. Surely they hadn't sunk to kippers? It must be smoked haddock. Not even this war could make the Fishwicks eat kippers for their main course.

She took off her slippers and, remembering her bootless floating up the aisle of the church, tiptoed downstairs. She held her breath going past the drawing-room door, but it remained shut. She popped her head around the door of the nursery, put her finger on her lips to Fanny, and slipped in.

Fanny grinned, and said in a loud voice, 'Now, Edwin dearie, just finish up this last bit of tapioca and then we can try again with our beef tea.' Then, in a whisper, 'Miss Dora, your Mother'll have your hide if she catches you in here. You were sent up till dinner time.'

''On't like beef tea,' said Edwin stoutly.

'I can't stay up there, Fanny, I'm too excited.'

'Well, it's beef tea or you go hungry, young man. That vicar's boy taken your fancy, then?'

'Ssh!' But Edwin started to howl at the prospect of either beef tea or hunger, so Dora relaxed. 'Fanny,' she said, standing in the middle of the room in a pose, 'look at me.'

Fanny paused, spoon poised between her and Edwin's high chair. 'Very nice, I must say, Miss Dora, but what's special about . . . Edwin! Now look, it's all down my clean apron! If you were mine I'd give you a . . . I'll tell your mam, I will!'

'Don't call Mother that, Fanny, *please*. Now, look at me. Do I seem . . . sort of . . . grown up, to you? I mean, I'm fifteen, nearly sixteen. Do I look, well, you know what I mean. . . .'

'You look quite developed, if that's what you're talking about,' said Fanny, concentrating more on dabbing her apron with a frayed handkerchief than on Dora's figure. 'You go in and out, sort of thing, like girls should when they're your age.'

'But. . . .'

'Whisper!'

'But,' Dora whispered, 'do I seem, well, you know, *grown up*?'

'Come on then, my boy, let's get rid of those tears and try again.' Now Fanny dabbed at Edwin with the same frayed handkerchief. 'Well, I think so, Miss Dora, I mean you seem to know a lot for your age.'

'Oh, I don't mean *that*!' Dora despaired. How could she ever make Fanny understand? And if Fanny didn't understand, who would?

Fanny got up and picked Edwin out of his high chair. 'Look, Miss Dora, if I were you I'd slip in to your mother and say you're sorry for having lost that cover and kept Edwin out in the snow for so long. She'll soften, she always does. Now, my boy, let's get you up to the bedroom and see if we can sort you out.'

And a nice get-out that'll be for you, thought Dora, if I take the blame! But as she watched Edwin's grubby face nuzzle into Fanny's neck as she carried him upstairs, she thought that it might not be such a bad idea after all. It would be warm in the drawing-room, anyway, which was more than it was in her bedroom, or even in the nursery, because Fanny had let the fire get low. Mother might scold, but Fanny was right, she usually did soften in the end. She sometimes even wept – whether for Dora's intractability or for some other reason, Dora did not know.

She went in quietly, and the heavy warm air hit her. The thick brocade yellow curtains were drawn, and logs and coal were heaped up on the fire. Mother sat in her usual winged armchair, hands folded wearily on her knee. She opened her eyes as Dora came in.

'I'm sorry, Mother.'

Her mother looked up, and then down disapprovingly at Dora's stockinged feet. But then she smiled a faint smile and put out her hand. She looked very tired.

Dora came and sat down at her feet, and leant against the chair. Her mother put a hand lightly on Dora's head. 'I wish Edwin wouldn't shriek so,' she said.

'He likes Fanny.'

'I know. But he can twist her around his little finger.'

'Yes.'

'If it isn't Edwin, it's Richard.'

Dora knew what her mother meant. Edwin would go to sleep, tomorrow would be another day, and who knows it might be one of his good, sunny days. But there were no sunny days for Richard.

'Your father said that it is coming up in Parliament today.'

'They're going to make him go?'

'Unless he is sick, or must support aged parents, or his work is of great importance to the nation.'

They both stared into the fire. Dora thought: Richard is perfectly fit, he couldn't support his parents even if they needed it, and his work is of no importance whatsoever.

She said, 'What will they do with him?'

'He will have to go before a tribunal.'

'A tri.... Like Lord Derby's tribunals? But Father....'

'I know, Dora. We will just have to hope he doesn't come before your father.' She sighed deeply. 'Perhaps Parliament will throw it out. But it will not throw it out. I know it.'

Dinner began in silence, apart, of course, from grace. When Father came out with the unimaginative 'Lord, bless this food to our use, and us in Thy service, Amen' she knew his mind was not on it. She wondered whether Mother had told him yet about her keeping Edwin out in a snowstorm. But it seemed she had not; probably they were both brooding about Richard. Dora nursed in her heart a glorious picture of the expressions on their faces if they were to know exactly where she had spent part of that snowstorm. Words rose in her mind as she supped her weak broth: 'Mrs Fishwick fell immediately into a swoon. Mr Fishwick stared, coloured, doubted and was silent. Could this be the daughter whose nonconformist soul he had nurtured so tenderly all these years?'

She watched Richard, contemptuously. Imagine if Humphrey Bosanquet were sitting there in his place! Home on leave, entertaining Father with tales from the trenches. . . . 'Sir Douglas was saying to me the other day – Haig, of course – that the Boche are on their last gasp. It's been tough, but the men have been heroic, simply heroic.'

'And you, too, dear boy,' Father would say. 'Do not hide from us your own gallant deeds.'

'Well, sir, I hesitate to tell you, but there was an occasion when I stepped out into No-Man's-Land amid heavy artillery fire from Messrs Hun to rescue a wounded fellow officer.'

Richard's voice sliced through Humphrey's words and made her spill her soup on to the tablecloth. 'I expect you know it has been discussed in the House today, Father.'

'Oh, Richard, how can you be so stupid!'

'Hush, Winifred. I am well aware of the introduction of the Military Service Bill, Richard.'

'Do you think it will go through, sir?'

'Since your own future depends on it, Richard, you would be well advised to make your own assessment of that.'

Dora said, 'But how can they *make* him fight? Even if they put a rifle in his hand, they can't make him pull the. . . .'

'Dora! If you abuse the privilege of this table you will go back to nursery tea!'

'Yes, Father.'

'And do not look at me like that. Richard, have you been reciting that prayer I gave you?'

'Yes, Father.'

'Every night?'

'Yes, Father.'

Dora watched Richard again. He really was extremely irritating. There were times when she found it almost impossible to despise him. Just now, he had finished his soup and was looking Father straight in the eye. Lizzie came in and removed the soup-bowls. Her slippered feet padded back along the corridor, jangling the bowls. *Crash* went the bowls into the sink in the butler's pantry: Mother's lips pursed sharply. Lizzie could be heard padding to the kitchen for the smoked haddock.

Richard said, 'Thou shalt not kill.' He sounded very pompous. Dora nearly laughed. She did not dare look at her father, but fixed her eyes on the tablecloth where she had spilt a little trail of pale brown broth.

Lizzie came back with the plates and a dish of boiled potatoes.

'I am sorry, Father. Tribunal or no tribunal, I cannot change my mind.'

'Richard!' Father, black with anger, indicated Lizzie.

But Richard said, 'Lizzie surely knows about my attitudes by now, don't you, Lizzie?' Lizzie did not look at him. 'You know that I would not kill another human being, whether he be German or nigger or yellow Mandarin. We are all God's creatures, are we not?'

Dora almost envied him. If only she could find an issue like this on which to defy Father!

Lizzie was pretending not to have heard what Richard said. Her expression was as stolid as ever. There was silence until she had brought in the main dish and the swede and left, closing the door noisily behind her.

'It's all so *colourless*,' said Mother, sounding peevish after Richard's whole-hearted passion. 'Look – white sauce on pale yellow fish, white potatoes and pale yellow swede. The soup was almost as bad.'

'Winifred!'

'I'm sorry, Arnold. I know it's the war. But if you had had a day like I have had with Edwin. . . .' She petered out.

'Richard,' said Father in a voice that forbade argument,

'I will not have you talking Socialism in front of the servants.'

'It is not Socialism, Father. It is Christianity.'

'I will not have you talking like that in front of the servants! Do you hear me!' Dora had just passed him his plate of fish and hoped his fist would come straight down into it. But it did not.

'If you say so, Father.'

There were the glimmerings of defeat in Father's eyes. 'Do you still defy me?'

'I refuse to put myself in a position where I might have to kill another human being.'

'You refuse to put yourself in a position where you might *yourself* be killed.'

'Those are your words, Father.'

Dora remembered saying to Fanny as they walked through the forbidden churchyard, 'Yellow as the drawing-room curtains.' She felt quite weary at the prospect of having to reconsider her judgment. No, he *was* a coward. It was just that he enjoyed defying Father. Well, who wouldn't?

There were lots of bones in her fish. Father didn't seem to have any. Did he crunch them between his big grey teeth, or swallow them whole? Richard and Mother took them out of their mouths, equally elegant as they did it, and put them carefully on the edge of their plates. Dora got one stuck between her teeth, and had to tug rudely to get it out. If Father noticed, she would say, 'What do you expect me to do with it? Choke on it?' Father didn't notice.

As they were silently eating their marmalade pudding, Dora looked with sudden interest at the encyclopaedia in the glass-fronted bookcase to the left of the fire. Her father consulted it on so many matters – perhaps there was something in there to enlighten her on this? She would have a look after dinner. She could pretend to be studying the South African War.

But no, after dinner Mother wanted her to hem handkerchiefs for the Comforts Fund. This horrible war spoils everything, she thought. No new winter bonnet, not enough servants to run the house properly, scrambled egg eked out with water, endless swede, Richard making a nuisance of himself, Father saying it was our duty to suffer as our lads were suffering in Flanders fields. . . .

But there was always Humphrey. She pressed the needle rhythmically with her thimble and thought of Humphrey. He rose between her and the handkerchief, black eyes blazing, lips slightly parted, looking like an adventure book hero with a touch of Rupert Brooke. 'Ah, God be thanked, who has matched us with His hour, And summoned us, as swimmers into cleanness leaping – ' How did it go on? 'Rats, and lice, and bits of men' – no, no, ugly ugly words, unworthy of Rupert Brooke or Humphrey Bosanquet, worthy only of puny young Alfred or Richard the worm.

Well, Richard the worm could look after himself. But she must cultivate puny young Alfred. It was through Alfred that Dora would meet at last her prince, her warrior lover, her fate.

Three

THE CLIMATE, however, was not conducive to the cultivation of Alfred Bosanquet. Snow followed snow, then a deep, cutting frost, and finally a grey slushy thaw. Edwin, moreover, developed an alarming hoarse cough.

'Croup!' cried Mother. 'And no wonder, the weather he has been exposed to!'

Dora watched Lizzie, Fanny and her mother leaning over Edwin, standing back, wiping their foreheads, dipping into out-of-date editions of *Bull's Maternal Management* and *Consult Me,* and recommending to each other mustard plasters, emetics, warm baths, leeches and tartarised antimony. She wondered how she would feel if Edwin were, of a sudden, wrenched untimely from them and flown to his rest on the bosom of Abraham. Would she be haunted by guilt? Perhaps his ghost would *tap-tap* on her door at night: she would hear his hoarse cough faintly on the stairs at midnight. She would be racked by grief, surely? Sitting white-faced on the sofa, dabbing at her eyes gently with a lace handkerchief, refusing food, driving her stricken parents insane with anxiety. But what if she felt nothing except relief? With no Edwin, Mother would sit and read *Ivanhoe* with her again. But no Edwin would mean no Fanny – which brought her back to Alfred Bosanquet. Time was passing; the Christmas holiday would soon be over; she would again have to go daily to Miss Gossage's, and there would be no more outings with Fanny and the perambulator for three whole months.

Doctor Fuller came and said that Edwin did not have croup. Lizzie returned to the kitchen, Mother to the drawing-room, and Fanny to bribing Edwin to eat his tea. But the cold weather prevailed, and it was not until the day before Miss Gossage's school opened for the spring term that it was mild enough for Edwin to take the air for more than a brief visit to the grocer's on the main road.

At breakfast, Mother said, 'Eat your porridge, Richard dear. Arnold, I think we can safely say that Edwin is now recovered.'

Father was reading the *Yorkshire Post*.

'Arnold, my dear, I need your advice.'

'Hm?'

'Arnold, I wish to consult you on a disciplinary matter.'

The anxiety in Mother's voice prevailed at last over the *Post*. 'Disciplinary? What is it, my dear?'

'Ah! Arnold – if Edwin goes out in the perambulator this afternoon with Fanny, do you think that Dora might accompany them? Richard, you have scarcely touched that porridge. You know that the country cannot afford waste.'

'I'm sorry, Mother. I seem to have lost my appetite.' Richard, indeed, had been eating very little lately. His clothes were beginning to hang on him like the loose covers on the chairs.

'Eat that up immediately, Richard,' said Father sharply. 'What an example to set your sister!'

Richard glanced at Dora, and then made another attempt on his porridge. Such meekness, she thought. I hope it chokes him. She looked at Father to see if he had forgotten Mother's enquiry. In fact, he was staring at her steadily, obviously in one of his inquisitorial moods.

'Have you apologized to your mother for the incident, Dora?'

'Yes, Father.'

'Have you prayed nightly and at each chapel attendance for Edwin's return to health?'

'Yes, Father.'

‘Have you done all in your power to help your mother and Fanny to tend Edwin in his distress?’

‘I – er – got up in the night to him’ – actually to go and shut his door to minimize the disturbance – ‘and fetched the mustard to Fanny for the footbath.’ This last was true. In return, Fanny agreed to tell her more of her grandfather’s adventures in the Crimean War.

‘Very well,’ said Father gravely. ‘I think Dora may be allowed a small expedition, Winifred.’

Dora breathed easily. She was careful not to smile.

‘Oh, I am glad, Arnold, because she is to go back to Miss Gossage’s tomorrow, and she *will* have her head down in books so, and she does need to take some fresh air or she gets such catarrh. . . . Richard, oh Richard, do eat it, you worry me so!’

‘I have eaten nearly half, Mother. I’m afraid the helping was a little large for me.’

Father rose. ‘We will discuss your appetite as we walk, Richard. Here is Lizzie with the eggs – please do not cause me to be late at the Shop.’

‘He won’t be there anyway.’ Dora was filled with gloom as they trudged again up the hill. It was one of those dismal dank January days when nothing romantic could possibly happen. Her mind’s eye glimpsed the tragic hopelessness that would sweep over her if the church were empty. It was a feeling that tempted her greatly. The alternative feeling, infinitely less attractive, was one of alarm lest something else should be going on in the church, something strange and sacred which might inflict the direst punishments on intruders.

‘Likely not,’ said Fanny composedly. ‘Let’s rattle the poor box and see what’s in it.’

‘I wish I was like you, Fanny – no morals at all.’

‘Miss Dora! Morals? I’ve plenty of *them*, thank you very much. But if I’m not poor, who is? Last week I spent half my savings on a new camisole. Well, I needed it. I know it’s a bit more frilly than suits my station, but, well, who’d miss a few coppers as we could squeeze out of the slot of the poor box, I ask you?'

This confirmed Dora in her plan to send Fanny and Edwin to the Green while she went alone to the church. She did not want undignified rattles echoing up to the rafters while she learnt the difference in tone of the swell and the great manuals and what heroic deeds Humphrey had been doing lately on the Western Front. Fanny was displeased, but Dora had only to exercise a little authority to get her to comply. They arranged to meet at the churchyard gate when the clock struck three.

She left her boots in the porch. She wanted to feel again the cold hard stone through her stockings, and to keep an element of surprise on her side. She closed the inner door quietly, and stood still for a moment to recapture the sensation of awe. Here she had come, deliberately, wilfully, to the beautiful and forbidden place, to meet the young stranger whose very existence was ignored by her family. 'Alfred!' she thought. 'Alfred – wherefore art. . . .' But how trite. Echoes of Montague and Capulet there were, yes, but hers was no time-worn plot. Her story, the story of Dora Fishwick, had never been written or even dreamed of before. In any case, it was not Alfred who was to be her Romeo, Alfred with his timidity and his receding chin. It was Humphrey – moustached (she was sure he had a moustache, a neat, aristocratic moustache like Sir Douglas Haig's), red-tabbed and shining-eyed, who was waiting in the wings of her stage.

The stained glass looked duller this time. It must be the leaden weather. And today there were no candles flickering above the organ, and no music playing.

She walked up the aisle slowly, silently, trying to ward off an unpleasant feeling of anti-climax. As she faced the altar, with its embroidered cloth and ornate gold crosses, she thought momentarily of God. The God who lived here received rich, formal, repetitive prayer. The God who lived at chapel got more variety – but did He miss the eloquence, the unity of voice, the weight of centuries of authority? The God who listened in these rafters must be a very orderly and ancient one. He would know exactly what was what. He wouldn't thrash about endlessly over moral problems like Mr Lofthouse's God at the chapel seemed to do. This God would be stalwart against cowardice, upright as a pillar in the midst of pettiness and vice.

Not daring to peer into the choir-stalls, still less venture up the steps into the pulpit, she tiptoed again towards the dark organ. She began to feel nervous. Perhaps the eye of that upright God was following her, waiting for the moment to send his minions to confront her. . . .

The organ bench was empty. She had visualized Alfred Bosanquet sitting there, hands on lap in the darkness, waiting patiently for her return. The emptiness of the bench was a severe shock. She stood there for several minutes, registering it.

Then she looked at the manuals, the stops and the pedals. They seemed to stare back at her, asking to be played. She gathered up her skirts and scrambled on to the bench, not caring now about noise. The pedals rattled as her stockinged feet pressed and then released them. She sat, looked round, pulled out a stop or two. *Diapason* – that she remembered well – *viola da gamba, dulcet, oboe.* Then, quickly, she pulled out every single one of them. What a marvellous blast of sound she could create if only that red-faced little boy were doing his job in the vestry!

She flicked through the hymn-book to find a tune that was familiar to her. Most of them were not; it was rather unnerving. Ah! *Old Hundredth.* She had played that on the piano at home. Wishing only that she knew how to use the pedals as well, she put her fingers on the nearest manual and began to play.

She was in full voice – 'Oh, enter then His gates – with – praise! A-pproach with joy his courts – un – to' – and making a mental note to tell Miss Gossage that here was a sentence ending in a preposition, when she was aware of someone standing near her. Terrified, she went on singing, fingers soundlessly hitting wrong notes, until the end of the verse – 'For – it is seem – ly so – to – do' – but her voice choked oddly on the 'do' and she turned abruptly and stared to her left, just as Alfred Bosanquet had done.

It was the vicar. Rector. (Tithes impropriate; tithes not impropriate?) It couldn't possibly be anyone else. Dora remembered that Fanny had depicted him as black, but her immediate impression of him was grey: slate-grey hair all thick and smooth, grey moustache (Kitchener-type, not Haig) and a steely face in between. He was standing absolutely still, looking affronted, shocked, astounded, incredulous – except that none of these emotions seemed actually to register themselves on his face. His expression was impassive, but he radiated condemnation.

Dora was stabbed with guilt. She wanted to die. Her mouth was still open from singing, but no sound came out.

The rector said, 'May I be so bold as to enquire your identity, and just what you consider you are doing desecrating the silence of my church?'

It occurred to Dora that the best thing she could do would be to burst into tears. But infuriatingly she couldn't summon any. She could only stammer, 'I met someone – a boy, well, I think he was your son – he told me about, he showed me the organ, it's lovely, I wanted to play it. . . .'

His voice like a knife-blade cut her off sharp. 'I think you are not a member of my congregation?'

'Er – no.' She thought it safer not to mention that she belonged to a rival organization.

'Have you any right to be here?'

'No – no.'

'Where and when did you meet my son – my younger son?'

'Here.'

'Why? How?'

'I – we – happened to take shelter from the snow in the porch. . . .'

'This is not one of General Booth's establishments, dispensing soup and succour. It is the house of God!'

'But I was singing a hymn!' Dora was astounded at her audacity – but really, Mr Lofthouse at the chapel would have congratulated her on her piety, whereas here was this joyless rector implying that she was guilty of the gravest profanities. ' "Approach with joy his courts unto" – that's what I was singing!'

'Indeed!' They were glaring at each other. Dora thought that he must surely want to laugh. The thing was so ridiculous. Was it there, the glimmer of a smile? Yes? No. 'There is a time for singing,' he said gravely, 'and a time for silence. A time for dancing, and a time for mourning – a time for peace, and a time for war.'

'It's the other way round.'

'I beg your pardon?'

'Mourning comes before dancing. In Ecclesiastes. And war before peace. I don't think singing comes in at all.' Oh, what a surge of power! She was right, she was sure of it!

The rector's expression changed oddly, and he moved his hands. She suddenly realized that he had been holding some small, flimsy sheets of paper in his right hand, and now they were fluttering to the ground. The rector bent quickly to pick them up. She could feel his confusion. One piece of paper had fallen on to the pedals, and she bent towards it. His hand and hers reached it at the same moment; he snatched it, but not before she had seen the letter-heading:

'2nd Yorks and Lancs.
B.E.F. France.'

'Oh!' she cried. 'It's from Humphrey!'

'Child!' The word shocked her, for it held genuine emotion. The sheets of paper rustled in his hand. He was trembling, and a little breathless.

She said quickly, 'I know about Humphrey – your elder son, I mean. Alfred told me all about him, about his being in the York and Lancaster Regiment and perhaps going to be made a full lieutenant and all the marvellously brave things he has done. . . .'

'Such as?' He was back to the knife-thrust, though still a little breathless.

All at once she realized that Alfred had not actually told her about any heroic deeds. She could remember only vague words about gallantry and leadership. 'Well, it's true, isn't it?'

There came a strange warmth and relaxation in the man's manner. 'Yes, my son is with the York and Lancaster on the Western Front. I have no doubt that a decoration will be coming his way before long. I am glad that Alfred shows such brotherly pride.' He held out a hand. 'Come down from that bench, young lady. You had better tell me your name, at any rate, before I send you packing.'

She was too scared to take his hand, but got off the organ bench gingerly and stood beside him. 'My name is Dora Fishwick.'

'Ah! Of course, of course. You are one of Mr Lofthouse's United Methodists. I have met your father, briefly. A respectable man.' A grave smile. 'He would not like to think you are in this sacred place, talking to the parish priest.'

'No.'

'And,' he went on, suddenly stiff, 'you have a brother? Humphrey's age – a little younger? Is he, too, with he York and Lancaster?'

Dora knew that it was of extreme importance to keep Richard out of the conversation. 'No – he, he – but where is Alfred? I though he might teach me more about the organ.'

'Alfred is at school. He returned yesterday.'

Of course. She could see the train steaming away, with Alfred sitting palely in a corner seat, feeling sick. 'Oh, I see. Please – please could you tell me more about Humphrey? I would really love to hear.'

'Shall I read you some of his letter?'

This surprised her. Letters were private, surely. But all the more delicious for being so. Thrilled, she said, 'Oh, yes, please! Where is he now? Has he been wounded? Where will the next big battle be, do you think? How long before the Huns are licked?'

Four

DORA WROTE: 'To the passer-by, Miss Gossage's College for Young Ladies looked like a haven of comfort and repose. But which of those onlookers, watching the neat black-stockinged girls ascend the broad steps each morning, could have realized what anguish of unending toil each girl must suffer under Miss Gossage's dictatorial rule?'

Lies, of course. But who would read *Jane Eyre* if Lowood had housed healthy and contented pupils? Dora did not in fact allow anyone to read her diary, and hid it every night under her pillow. But she was certain it would be found 'amongst her papers' when she died (tragically, so young – or heroically, after a painful illness bravely and beautifully borne) and published under a pseudonym.

Miss Gossage's school had been opened recently in one of the villas of delapidated grandeur which stood along the road towards town, in the opposite direction from the church and the Green. She gathered pupils without difficulty, for her original girls recommended her to all their friends. The difficulty where Dora was concerned was for her mother to persuade her father that she needed a broader education than Mrs Lofthouse could provide each morning at the manse.

'The breadth of Dora's education,' Father had said, 'is gained in her evening discussions with me.' As indeed it had been. Mrs Lofthouse could only offer embroidery, elementary arithmetic and the recitation of poetry. But Father had lectured her every Tuesday and Thursday, for three-quarters of an hour before she had her cocoa, on the causes of the Indian Mutiny, the invention of electricity, the military manoeuvres at the Battle of Waterloo, the lives of John and Charles Wesley, mediaeval herbal remedies, or any other subject on which his fast-moving mind had happened to alight at the time. Years before, he had attempted the same sort of instruction on Richard. But Richard had shuffled and yawned and once actually dropped off to sleep, at which Father gave up, deeply hurt. Dora knew that she had been second best for these sessions. But her absorbed attention and pertinent questions had gradually softened Father's bitterness, and the original half-hour had been lengthened to three-quarters as a mark of special praise.

The war, of course, had changed everything. Father had become preoccupied with staff and trade problems at the Shop, and with Richard at home. Edwin's arrival and his sabotage of Mother's peace of mind made Father more pliable. And, most significantly, Mrs Lofthouse was out of favour. The Lofthouses were all out of favour. No one actually said so, but Dora knew that it was so. Nobody could sit by Mother and Father in chapel twice every Sunday and fail to sense them stiffening in vain fury.

Dora missed the evening sessions with Father, but was pleased to exchange kind but scatty Mrs Lofthouse for vigorous Miss Gossage. The greatest loss in the whole business was the loss of Phoebe.

Even Richard realized this. 'I'm sorry about Phoebe, Dora,' he had said on one of their Sunday afternoon walks last summer when Father was striding far in front of them. Dora had wanted to say, 'It's all *your* fault,' in the way she'd used to in quarrels with Richard. But this new Richard, who worked at the Shop and gained his moral attitudes elsewhere than from Father, forbade such rudeness. She said stiffly, 'I can live without Phoebe,' and increased her pace to catch up with Father.

Living without Phoebe was actually harder than she had expected. She and Phoebe Lofthouse had studied and prayed and giggled together since Phoebe's father had come to the chapel six years ago. There was no one among the bright, easy-going girls at Miss Gossage's to replace her. There was Betsy Fuller, the doctor's daughter, a puny girl with lank hair who followed Dora around hoping to get her sums done, and Minnie Chapman, whose sophisticated tastes Dora greatly admired. But there was nobody she could share a secret with as she could with Phoebe, nobody who could mock her with impunity like Phoebe, no one to tease and quarrel with and then make it up and feel better than before.

'Girls!' said Miss Gossage brightly. 'Back to Bloody Mary! Put down your slates and listen to the story.'

The girls chattered and settled. Miss Gossage opened a book, cleared her throat, and began to read: ' "It was not very long before some of the Protestants, and others who disliked Queen Mary, raised a rebellion against her; and the Queen, suspecting that Elizabeth might be in some way concerned in this rebellion. . . ." '

Dora noticed a small pile of books on Miss Gossage's table. The table was, as usual, extremely untidy. Dora could count three bottles of ink, at least seven pens, two crumpled lace handkerchiefs, and innumerable hairpins which were apt to fall out of Miss Gossage's bun. But the books, she knew, were for her. Was one of them the promised Tolstoy? Miss Gossage had said before Christmas, 'I wonder if you are ready for Tolstoy, Dora?' By which Dora understood Tolstoy to be an author who was mature, mysterious, and probably frowned upon by her father.

Later, Miss Gossage set the older girls a composition while she helped the younger ones with their grammar and spelling. She gave the subject: 'I was burnt at the stake under Mary Tudor'.

Normally Dora would have scribbled happily on brutal priests, licking flames, and hearts throbbing among the dying embers. Today, however, she preferred to think about Humphrey. She could remember his letter almost word for word, and wanted to write it down before she forgot it. She would tell Miss Gossage that she had a headache.

'2nd Yorks and Lancs.,' she wrote. 'British Expeditionary Forces, France.' The rector had explained that they were not allowed to say exactly where they were, for fear of the Boche finding out. Some of them invented elaborate codes, like 'P.S. I am a Young Person Really Eager to Serve', when they were at Ypres. Humphrey thought this practice underhand and dishonourable. 'Dear Father,' he had written, 'thank you for your letter. I was sorry to hear about old Mr Whittington. In him you have lost a valuable and long-serving choir-member.' Dora found this a less than exciting opening to her first letter from the Front. But of course Humphrey would be deeply loyal to his father and reluctant to launch into his own more dramatic concerns. 'I am in a splendid billet here. I have washed and shaved, and in my clean clothes I feel as fit as a fiddle.' So much for Alfred's rats and lice. 'We had a Divisional Inspection by the Corps Commander yesterday, and have been doing some route marches of ten miles. We get some good riding on our afternoons off. The air is very bracing. I would be very grateful if you could send biscuits, candles and a tin of Colgate's shaving powder. Give my love to Mother, and good wishes for her return to health. Your affectionate son, Humphrey.'

Dora's hand hovered over the paper when she approached the tin of Colgate's shaving powder. It seemed so mundane, so domestic and unheroic. But honesty must prevail. Even heroes must shave. She wrote on to the end.

On the whole, she thought, it was a letter from a modest and courageous man. 'Fit as a fiddle' must mean 'Do not worry on my account, Father. I may live my life in constant danger, but my spirits are high'. 'Divisional Inspection . . . route marches . . . riding' – behind these words lay heavy responsibility and a stern discipline. 'The air is bracing': how like him to pass off life at the Western Front as if it were a spring holiday in Scarborough!

The concluding concern for his mother tied up with Alfred's mention of Mrs Bosanquet's nervous complaints. Clearly she was not able at the moment even to attend to his requests for everyday items such as biscuits or candles. Did she get letters from Humphrey addressed particularly to her, as this was addressed to 'Dear Father'? Surely the ailing Mrs Bosanquet could not be excluded entirely, except for a brief message, from her son's correspondence?

There was no mention of wounds, dead comrades, or even of the enemy. Dora had to stifle her disappointment. But of course, he was not in the trenches at the moment. His father said that they had periods in the trenches and periods of rest, and this letter was written during one of the periods of rest.

Betsy Fuller shifted on her chair and tried to look over at Dora's composition. Dora moved her elbow further around her writing and lowered her head. Her heart had begun to pound at the memory of what the rector had said next: 'Perhaps you would like to come here and play the organ sometimes? And I could show you Humphrey's letters, if you are interested.' If only she could. She had murmured something about hoping it would be possible, at which he had suddenly become very formal and said that his time was more than taken up with parish duties – though he usually stayed in the church on saints' days, after the sacrament of holy communion. She wondered if he would prevail upon the unfortunate choirboy to go on pumping in the vestry for her benefit. Or maybe his absence would be an excuse to get down the more quickly to the business which concerned them both: that of poring over Humphrey's letters.

Miss Gossage accepted Dora's headache without question, but gave her no sympathy. Miss Gossage had no time for illness. Betsy Fuller constantly had catarrh, chilblains and cramps, but Miss Gossage's reaction was usually a brisk, 'Well, doctors' children die first, so they say, Betsy – a morning's map-drawing will soon put it out of your head.'

Tolstoy was not among the books. Instead, Miss Gossage had collected some titles 'more suitable to your age than those dreadful Marie Corelli romances you have been reading lately'. But she added with a sidelong smile that though she recommended the American ladies for their brightness and sincerity, she had a feeling that Mr Haggard and Mr Kipling might take Dora's fancy most.

At home, Dora carried the books quickly up to her room. She decided at a glance that Susan Coolidge and Louisa M. Alcott were suitable to take down and read in the drawing-room. Father might approve of H. Rider Haggard's opening 'Now glory be to God who has given us the victory', but to follow it with torture and slavery and the dishonouring of daughters within the first paragraph was a certain recipe for confiscation. The small blue Kipling, oddly titled *Stalky and Co,* was not after all about a shop but about some boys who talked in a strange mixture of French and Latin and English and seemed to behave like gypsies imitating General Baden-Powell. These two books would need more careful and discreet study than the two girls' ones, and must wait until later.

Mother was in the kitchen discussing dinner and Edwin with Lizzie and Fanny, so she had the drawing-room to herself. The fire was sizzling brightly; Mother had left the lights turned up full and Lizzie had been in to draw the curtains. Dora lay down on her stomach in front of the fire and opened *Little Women.*

Half an hour later, impatiently thrusting it to one side and opening *What Katy Did,* she was beginning to wonder whether all American girls had as many sisters as did Jo and Katy. Did their parents *allow* them to argue and insult one another, and wander about the countryside with no one to mind them? It wasn't as if they were Godless people – they were endlessly playing pilgrims – but the way they all play-acted and climbed trees and. . . .

Suddenly the front door banged. Dora sat up. Who

could it be? Lizzie and Fanny never went out on errands in the dark in winter. Mother certainly was at home. And with Father and Richard at the Shop. . . .

Richard came in quickly and closed the door. He was breathing heavily, and despite having been out in the cold wind his face was very pale.

'Oh, you're here, Dora.' He seemed relieved. 'Where's Mother?'

'In the kitchen. But why have you come home? It's only. . . .'

Richard slumped down in Father's chair. 'I know it's only. What time is it, actually? Oh, ten to five. I've come up against it at the Shop.'

Dora hugged her knees and looked curiously at him. 'What happened? Has Father thrown you out?'

'Oh, Dora, you're so dramatic. It was all very sordid really. Grimes from leather goods came to Father and said he thought he ought to volunteer. A neighbour of his has come home wounded and he thinks that 'a man for a man' is the only way we could . . . could smash the beastly Hun, he said. Father said he respected that, though it would mean taking on another female member of staff which he didn't like doing. Then Grimes looked at me and said, "I understand that Mr Simpson three doors from you in Heathgate has had an unfortunate telegram about his son, sir. A man for a man, that's my philosophy, sir – and you say you agree with it, sir?" Talking to Father but all the time looking at me.'

'What could you say to that?'

'You can't get at me, you know, Dora.' He grinned a little. 'What I could say, and did say, was that I felt war to be against Christian principles, and that I was prepared to go to prison if need be for the sake of my conscience.'

'Prison!'

'Of course. Didn't you realize that? But I couldn't expect you to understand. Anyway, Mr Grimes certainly didn't understand. He went a bit wild, and asked Father how he could stand there and let a lily-livered coward like me try to put him in the wrong – and then he realized what he was saying and stood stammering like a child and saying that all he wanted was to get to the Front and defend his womenfolk like any man should. He went on like that for some time, apologizing and whining and begging to be allowed to go. Father didn't seem able to stop him. I think he was embarrassed because I was there. Eventually he turned to me and said that I should go home. Just like that.'

'So you did?'

'So I did. And he said as I left that he would see me later about when I should return to work.'

'You're not to go back until he says so?'

'No. Well, I cause trouble, don't I? If I go down to haberdashery to check the accounts, there's Mr Maynard, whose son was killed at Ypres. In footwear there's Miss Hankinson who took the place of Mr Yeomans who enlisted and was then lost at Gallipoli. Even old Trapnell at the door has two sons in the trenches. They hate me, I'm afraid, Dora. They simply hate me.'

Dora didn't know what to say. To her there seemed one simple solution to Richard's problem. She said abruptly, 'Do you know what it's like in the trenches, Richard?'

'Not really.' He sat forward and stared into the fire. She saw the fine scattering of dots on his face where he had shaved, and remembered his flash of pride two or three years ago when he had told her that he had shaved for the first time. 'All I know is that there's more to it than we read in the papers.' Richard was indeed reading the newspaper as carefully as Father these days. 'Judging by the lists of casualties and the little ground we've gained . . . . But it's pointless talking war with you, Dora. You'll only tattle about it to your schoolgirl friends. What are you smiling about?'

'Oh,' answered Dora, 'I know more about the war than you think I do.'

'And how is that?'

'Mind your own business. Hadn't you better go and tell

Mother about what happened?'

A small victory gained, she thought proudly when Richard had left. Not that he seemed particularly interested in her secret. He was too wrapped up in nursing his own twisted conscience. She turned back to *What Katy Did,* but with little heart. She really wanted to know what Richard would do next. Why fight Mr Grimes and old Trapnell and Father and Mother, when the Germans were just over the Channel and deserved all they got?

She turned to the fire and felt it hot on her face. She thought of Humphrey, in front of a French fire crackling just like this one, and a sturdy old Frenchwoman at the range, cooking his dinner. She imagined herself as him, in khaki, kneeling battle-worn and weary and warming fingers that only hours ago had held a bloodstained bayonet. She saw the bayonet in the flames, streaked with German blood. . . .

Then the flames blurred. A wave of dizziness swept over her – she thought she was swaying towards the fire. Her head began to throb, and down in her stomach a disgusting sickness was swelling.

She swallowed quickly, made her body go rigid, closed her eyes and whispered through clenched teeth, 'God, let it go away. God, let it go away.'

The sickness eased, the throbbing faded. She stirred, knelt up straight, and congratulated herself shakily on the success of her will-power. But she was frightened. What had happened to her? Had it been the blood-stained bayonet in the flames? No, the sickness was not in her mind, it was in her body. She remembered the night about a month ago when she had woken in the darkness, sweating, and with that same swelling nausea. It was just after Christmas. She wondered if she had over-eaten, but they were never allowed to over-indulge, especially at Christmas. It was not her imagination, and it was not her digestion. Something was happening to her, and she did not understand it.

She stood up. She was still a little shaky, and her knees

felt strange. She had a sudden need to see her mother.

Opening the drawing-room door, she saw her mother carrying Edwin along the hall to the nursery. He was giggling, and Mother was half laughing too, saying breathlessly, 'Edwin, darling, now calm yourself a little or you'll never listen to the nice story I'm going to tell you if you. . . . Oh, Dora!' The way she said 'Oh, Dora!' as she passed told Dora that her mother was not communicating with anyone but Edwin at the moment. Where was Richard? Cowardly as usual, he must have gone up to his room.

She said, 'I'm just going upstairs, Mother,' but she paused on the bottom stair, holding on to the banister, until Mother and Edwin were safely in the nursery. Then she went along to kitchen.

Lizzie and Fanny were talking, but stopped as soon as Dora came into the room. Lizzie was rolling pastry, Fanny was holding in her red hands the remains of Edwin's tea. Dora looked from one to the other and said, 'I felt a little faint in the drawing-room a moment or two ago. In fact, I've felt faint several times lately.'

'Well!' Lizzie looked at Fanny and Fanny looked at Lizzie.

'That,' said Fanny, 'tells me a thing or two. Doesn't it tell you a thing or two, Lizzie? Felt a big green, did you? Well, well, it's only to be expected at your age. After all, you're soon to be sixteen, Miss Dora, aren't you? Feeling faint, and all that sort of thing.'

She and Lizzie might look sympathetic, but Dora knew they were laughing at her. She felt suddenly very well and very angry. 'Don't just stand there, both of you! Can't one of you get me a glass of water, or tell me to sit down, or something? Doesn't anyone care that I feel faint and I've got a headache?' She was shouting now. 'Don't you know what happened to Aunt Izzie when she had a headache? She died of typhoid fever! How would you like it if I died of typhoid fever?'

Then she burst into tears. She collapsed into a chair and

heard Fanny say to Lizzie over her head, 'Who's her Aunt Izzie?' Lizzie said, 'She ain't got one, far as I know.' Dora, still weeping, accepted a glass of water from Lizzie, and she cursed the one half of the world who had never read *What Katy Did* and the other half of the world who seemed incapable of understanding anything that Dora did.

Five

'BLESSED ARE YE,' cried Mr Lofthouse joyfully, 'when men shall revile you, and persecute you' – Dora thought of the church organ and of Mr Lofthouse pulling out a further stop for each reverberating phrase – 'and shall say all manner of evil against you falsely for my sake! Rejoice' – here he seemed to add a high four-foot stop so that he sounded like Miss Gossage in her Elizabethan fervour – 'and be exceeding glad, for great is your reward in heaven.' Mr Lofthouse's cheeks were pink, and his eyes were fixed on Richard.

Dora could imagine what had been going on at the manse recently: Richard, locked alternately in long prayer-sessions with the minister and long tea-sessions with the minister's wife, filling himself both with physical strength (for Mrs Lofthouse baked superb cakes, and even Richard could not resist them) and with spiritual strength to defy his father. While Phoebe . . . ? If only she could see Phoebe! She had absolutely no idea what Phoebe thought of Richard's scrimshanking. There had been a time when she had pictured Richard as the ideal mate, muted and gentle, for bright wild Phoebe. Phoebe used to say that Richard was like a spaniel, begging to be looked after. What confusion must this irritable, defiant new Richard be creating in Phoebe, as in Dora herself! Or might a defiant upstanding Richard be drawing out a new gentleness from Phoebe? The thought made Dora sick. She simply couldn't bear to think of Phoebe admiring Richard in that way.

Phoebe was sitting in the front pew on the opposite side, alongside her younger sisters and her mother. They sat very still; Dora hoped they were all stuck to the varnish. She herself was finding it more impossible every Sunday to sit still. Each week now as Father carved the shoulder of mutton (oh for some sirloin of beef, like in the old days!) he had delivered the same tedious homily on control of body, mind and soul.

Dora was sitting in between Father and Mother, and Richard sat on the far side of Mother. Richard was rapt. Mother's head was down, and she was fingering one of the buttons on her coat. Father's right leg was crossed over his left, but he was moving his right foot in a rather odd, rhythmical manner. Dora watched it for a while, fascinated. Then she found that by moving her head just a little to the left she could glance at Father's face without his being aware of it. She saw that it was creased in a deep, painful frown.

'Think of the first martyr, Stephen!' urged Mr Lofthouse. 'Think of his last words, echoing as they do the dying words of Christ Himself: "Lord, lay not this sin to their charge". Does this not give to us the supreme example, to love, even in the face of death, and to forgive our enemies?'

The sight of her father's frown moved Dora. For a moment she could imagine him when he was Richard's age. His face would have been much solider than Richard's, his chin jutting out as it did now and not sloping ignominiously away as Richard's did. How unfair of Fate to make her inherit that square face and resolute jaw, while giving to Richard, as male and heir, their mother's look of insubstantial refinement. Richard was hardly a son for a man like Father to be proud of. Rejected now even by the common employees in the Shop, was he spending his time in scholarly study or in exercising for physical fitness? No. Refusing service to his country and filial responsibility, he rode off on his bicycle to spend his empty hours with Mr Lofthouse, whom Father called a self-styled prophet who used his own misguided interpretation of the Scriptures to lead the youth of the country away from their patriotic duty to fight. Mother had objected to the description of Mr Lofthouse as a prophet on the grounds that his influence probably did not spread further than their own chapel. But Father had retorted that it had spread over the Fishwicks' threshold, and that was enough for him.

As Mr Lofthouse's exhortations rolled on, Dora wondered about Uncle Richard Fishwick. Uncle Richard had been older than Father. Father never spoke of him. When Mother talked about him, it was with deep reverence. 'Of course, Grandpapa Fishwick intended your uncle Richard to take over the Shop from him. But he went to South Africa and died there. So your father, of course, did his duty and took over the Shop.'

Dora wondered how he had died. Shot by a Zulu arrow? Boiled by cannibals – or did that happen only to missionaries? Perhaps ignominiously of enteric. Or even of a foul gangrenous wound, like the man in Fanny's grandad's story. Did he, as he lay screaming or vomiting, wish that he had stayed quietly at home, ordering toppers and lace-trimmed boleros and wondering if it would be improper for a United Methodist to stock ladies' bathing dresses?

The end of the sermon came suddenly. Dora was startled into rising to her feet for 'Guide me, O Thou great Jehovah'. She sang with pleasure, even though the tone of the chapel organ gave her pain. 'Bread of He – eaven, bread of He – eaven,' she sang, and prayed that one day she would be able to play this on the organ of St Dunstan's. To her surprise, she heard Richard singing lustily as well. He usually muttered, like Mother. 'Bid my anxious fears subside,' came along the pew to her as a heart-felt if toneless plea. 'Death of deaths, and he – ll's destruction' – grand words, whatever they meant – 'land me safe on Can – aan's side.' In a few moments they would be outside the chapel door, to face beaming Mr Lofthouse with hand outstretched. Would Father take it? Or would he pass by, frozen, without even a glance into the minister's pleading eyes?

'The padre is a good fellow,' wrote Humphrey. 'The men regard him as a veritable fountain of cigarettes.' Reverend Bosanquet laughed shortly as he turned over the page. Though she wanted to laugh too, Dora did not, partly because her parents had taught her to disapprove of cigarettes but mainly because she was very nervous.

She was only half-listening to Humphrey's letter, because it was so extraordinary that she should be here at all. She felt that surely the church warden or the organist or even, incredibly, Father would come in and surprise them in the act. In the act of what? Sitting on opposite sides of a rather shabby table on which lay Bibles, prayer-books and a concordance, talking not at all but reading quietly and undramatically from flimsy pieces of notepaper.

'Rumours reach us of activities in the trenches. It seems that Fritz is energetically disposed towards us at the moment.'

It was the day of the Purification of the Virgin Mary. Of all the facts of her situation, this near-Papist one would shock Father the most. Dora had asked Miss Gossage whether she could borrow an Anglican prayer-book. There was no reason why Miss Gossage should have such a thing, for she was a Quaker. Dora did not know much about Quakers, but she did know that they did not use prayer-books. However, Miss Gossage produced an Anglican prayer-book, advised her to read it only at school, but asked no questions.

The prayer-book told her what she wanted to know, which was the date of the next saint's day. It was the Presentation of Christ in the Temple, commonly called the Purification of Saint Mary the Virgin.

While she had waited for Fanny at the gate last time she was at the church, she had lifted a loose corner of the poster on the noticeboard ('To the Women of Britain' had gone; now it was 'Will you March too, or wait till March 2?') and read that Holy Communion on saints' days was at 10 am. How long would it last? Half an hour? An hour? She settled on 11 am as a time to go.

The next question was how to approach Miss Gossage. She could pretend illness – but Miss Gossage would either ignore it or, if she thought Dora's pallor to have a serious cause, ask Betsy Fuller to accompany her home. Or she could arrange to have dropped one of Miss Gossage's books on the path on the way to school. But the book she was borrowing at the moment was a bound edition of the *Girl's Own Paper* of 1894, which was lent out only as a particular favour. Dora could not bear to think of so misusing it.

Finally she settled on directness. 'I am interested in exploring other faiths,' she announced.

'How very interesting, Dora.' Miss Gossage patted the chair beside her desk, and Dora sat down. The other girls were drawing pictures of Shakespeare's Globe Theatre. 'Which faith particularly attracts you? Islam? Buddhism? Such a peaceful and undogmatic attitude, the Buddhist. Hinduism is rather complex. . . .'

'No, no. I meant the Church of England.'

'Church of *England*? That is a *denomination*. Established maybe, but only a denomination. Their sacramental wine is alcoholic, you know.'

'Oh!' This aspect had not struck Dora before, and lent additional excitement. Of course she would not actually partake of the intoxicating liquor. But she could not remember ever having been under the same roof as alcohol before now. 'No, I only want to visit the church, get the *feel* of it. I consider my background to have been rather restricted. Later I might go to the Wesleyans, and the Baptists, maybe to the Quakers too.'

'You thirst after religious experience, eh, Dora?' Dora was not quite sure that Miss Gossage was taking her seriously. 'Well, I see no reason why you should not take a walk on a fine day to one of the nearby churches. Which friend would you like to take with you?'

'I'd rather go alone, if you don't mind, Miss Gossage. I can't think of anyone who would be . . . suitable.' She held her breath.

So Miss Gossage's half-smiling 'Very well, Dora,' had become the *open sesame* to Humphrey's letters.

She stared at the cheap bits of paper in Reverend Bosanquet's hand. What was written on them still seemed very tame. If only Humphrey weren't so modest! If only he would write in detail about his daring exploits!

'Parades start at 7 am each day.' She would think of him as she pulled on her combinations. 'We have lectures in the evening on trench-digging, use of bayonets and machine-guns, etc.' Did he give the lectures or listen to them? 'One of our men, a little Private from Heckmondwike, has won the V.C. for bravery last November.' There followed a long description of what this little Private from Heckmondwike had done to deserve his decoration. Reverend Bosanquet was clearly editing it for Dora's benefit.

But Dora was not interested in the Private's exploits. She was trying to master a lump in her throat, which was a lump of fury. She was furious with her own nervousness, she was furious with Humphrey for parading and lecturing instead of fighting and suffering. Most of all she was furious with the Private from Heckmondwike who had gained the honour that only Humphrey justly deserved.

'With good wishes to all of you, your devoted Humphrey.' Mr Bosanquet seemed to take Dora's silence as a mark of respect rather than anger. 'Splendid, splendid. A V.C. in the regiment always reflects the quality of its officer material. Humphrey must be very proud.' He sat back, put the letter on top of a Bible, and stretched his grey, veined hands on the table. Dora stared at them, afraid to look at his face. The lump in her throat gave way to a preoccupation with what to say next. 'I always bring his letters here to the church to read,' he went on, with a hint of embarrassment. 'It – it upsets my wife, you see, to think of Humphrey in that situation. We don't speak of him at home. My wife . . . tends to fear the worst.'

His unease began to give Dora confidence. 'Does she not feel proud of his valour in the field?' she asked.

'Of course, of course. But great heroism can bring its own . . . consequences.'

They sat in silence for a moment. Reverend Bosanquet leant forward and started folding the pages of the letter neatly, pressing his finger carefully along the fold from one end to the other.

'I'm . . . I'm very grateful, sir,' Dora burst out, 'for the opportunity of sharing. . . .' She stopped, alarmed at the intimacy of the word 'sharing'.

He said stiffly, 'Receiving letters from the Front is a privilege I am glad to share.' He stood up. 'Now perhaps you should be returning to your studies? I presume you have made some explanation to your schoolmistress – have stretched the truth a little, perhaps?'

'I beg your pardon, sir? Oh, oh yes, I told her that I wished to explore other, er, denominations.' She pushed back her chair and stood up. 'Sir – you said that I might . . . might some day play the organ, like your son Alfred?'

'The organ? Oh yes, we did discuss that possibility. It would call for the services of young Liversidge at the bellows. . . . Or I might prevail upon our housekeeper's boy to perform. He has done so before in time of need. When would you require him?'

Dazed, Dora replied, 'Perhaps next week at about the same time?'

'I shall make enquiries and see what can be arranged.' He held out his hand over the table, and she took it briefly. It was cold, but then so was hers. 'Good morning, Miss Fishwick.'

She was dismissed. She felt almost that she should walk backwards out of the vestry. But she turned to go out, and then almost ran down the aisle. Then, when she had closed the church door firmly behind her, she began to skip. She skipped down the gravel path in the cold sunshine and went on skipping all the way down the hill until she was within yards of Miss Gossage's School for Young Ladies.

She skipped all the way home, too. She gulped down her bread and butter, did her piano practice without having to be reminded, and then went hot-foot to the nursery to confide in Fanny. She would not actually *tell* Fanny anything, she decided – but to be able to hint at dark secrets, to suggest dire crime and high adventure without divulging their nature would be sheer delight.

'Imagine, then, my confusion,' she wrote later that night, 'when I found Richard in the nursery. He was seated on one of the tiny chairs, sharing milk and honey sandwiches with Edwin. Fanny was behaving in an extraordinary manner in her effort to combine being an efficient nursemaid with being an engaging young lady.'

Dora decided to take no notice of Richard, and helped herself to a honey sandwich. Edwin was howling, because Fanny was too busy listening to Richard's objections to military service to attend to her charge's needs. Dora gave him a sandwich and sat back, determined to remain aloof.

'You see, Fanny, if I accept non-combatant service – that is, if I join one of the army's support battalions, who don't actually do any fighting – would I really be keeping my hands clean? Of course not! All I would be doing is to release one more man to fight at the Front!'

'But,' said Fanny, '*you* wouldn't actually be killing anybody.'

'But can't you see, Fanny, it makes no difference who pulls the trigger? If I said to you I want to steal, er, Father's watch, say – but I don't think it's right to steal, so will you take it for me – would that be right? Well, would it?'

'Well, no, no, of course it wouldn't, Mr Richard. I think I'm just beginning to see what you mean.'

Dora noticed with disgust the rapid disappearance of

Fanny's 'he's young, he's single and he's got to go' frame of mind. Edwin had had enough tea and was beginning to sing 'The Queen was in the parlour, counting bread and honey.' '*Eating* bread and honey,' Dora corrected him severely. 'No eating, finished eating,' said Edwin. Dora missed a stage in Richard's argument.

'I know all about that, Fanny. But don't you think they say the same about us? Now don't tell me about them rendering down corpses for tallow.'

'Mr Richard!'

'I'm sorry, Fanny, but they do say these things about the Germans. Yes, they do, Dora, and worse too. But they're not true. They're simply not true – or they're only as true as the German tales about us. We're all the same under the skin, you know. Take the Christmas truce of 1914.'

'But those were Saxons, not beastly Prussians!' broke in Dora, forgetting her resolution.

'Saxons, Prussians, Hanoverians, what does it matter, any more than Yorkshireman or Cockney to us? We're all *people*, Dora, can't you see? I'd no more thrust a bayonet into one of them than I would into you or Fanny!'

'Ah!' said Fanny suddenly, with a gleam in her eye, 'but what if one of them was to come and foully ravish and mutilate Miss Dora? What would you do *then*?'

Richard wavered. For a moment Dora thought he had no answer. But then he seemed to reach out for it, and he said with solemn triumph, 'I would pull him away, and offer to sacrifice myself in her place.'

Dora frowned, and turned to lift Edwin down. Would Richard really lay down his life for hers, as Dickens' Sydney Carton died on the scaffold for Charles Darnay? It was an appealing thought. But if he did that she would be left alone with the foul German, so her last state would be no better than her first. Was this what Richard intended?

'I bet you'll give in and go, in the end,' she said defiantly, 'when they come along to take you to prison.'

Richard straightened up. 'That remains to be seen.

Anyway, I've already made my application for exemption from military service.' He looked pleased at the expressions on their faces. 'Yes, in triplicate. I sent it off yesterday.'

'But what grounds have you given?'

'Conscientious grounds, of course. It's pointless my making excuses about health or work or family. The Military Service Act has a clause allowing for conscientious objection.'

'But Father says that hardly any tribunals are letting people off.'

'And he and his colleagues certainly aren't. You don't have to tell me, Dora. With such severe losses in both the English and French armies, they're going to try to get every possible man.' He picked up Edwin and put him on his knee. Edwin struggled to get down. 'Come on, Edwin, *you're* on my side, surely? No?' He let Edwin go, and Dora thought she saw his lip tremble. 'Well,' he said, 'whatever happens, I'm going to go through with it. I've no choice in the matter. It's simply something I've got to do.'

Six

PANSY. *We think you have more need of a doctor than of us; this is all we can gather from so incoherent a letter. We are at a loss to understand what you mean. You had better get medical advice. If you have left off prayer, no wonder you are miserable, and the sooner you begin again the better and happier for you.*

Dora speculated on what poor Pansy's trouble had been, but she could not summon up the names of all the intimate maladies which floated into her mind. Had Pansy died of it, whatever it was? If she had survived, having written to the *Girl's Own Paper* in 1894 when she was, perhaps, sixteen, she would be thirty-eight now! Had she, too, had regular fainting attacks? And what of 'Anxious One, No. 2' who was told, *A bad digestion is probably the cause of your trouble? What* trouble? How did the *Girl's Own Paper* expect its replies to be helpful to its other readers if . . . but of course, the questions may have been too indelicate to print.

Might she, now, write to the *Girl's Own Paper* herself? She would never dare.

She thought that she must return the volume to Miss Gossage without delay. She had had it for more than a month now, and it was a nuisance hiding it between her clean nightdresses in the drawer. Some of the articles in it were in fact extremely wholesome, and there was a seemly concentration on Bible study, neat handwriting and filial respect. But what would Father say to her reading about 'Girls' Attire: the Newest and Best' or advice to a young girl to write to the secretary of Girton College?

She was no nearer the solution to her problem, however. In fact, one day recently something had happened which she had long feared: she had fainted at Miss Gossage's, during a geography lesson. The girls were most impressed, and Miss Gossage even told Betsy Fuller to lend Dora her smelling salts. Dora had been kept in after school, so that Miss Gossage could probe her gently but firmly with questions.

It was the day after one of Dora's regular visits to the church, and Miss Gossage was not slow to make the connection. 'Tell me, Dora, in confidence – why are you so interested in religious matters?'

Dora, still feeling rather sick, found herself unable to reply.

'Presumably your parents do not know about your enquiries?'

Dora shook her head.

Miss Gossage sighed and tried a new line of attack. 'You have had these fainting attacks before? How often?'

'A few times, since Christmas.'

'Are they connected . . . with any other event?'

Dora thought she was referring again to her 'enquiries'. 'No, no, definitely not, Miss Gossage.'

'Well then.' Miss Gossage became brisk. 'If it happens again, either at home or at school, you are to tell me about it, Dora. You will do that? Good. And in the meanwhile I think you should lead a quieter life. No reading late at night when your parents think you are asleep!' Miss Gossage laughed, and Dora laughed too, from relief.

She felt almost well as she walked home. She could still go to St Dunstan's.

But for what? When she went for her first session at the organ, the candles were lit, the housekeeper's boy was waiting in the vestry, and there was a note on the vestry table to the effect that an organ student would be at practice from eleven o'clock that morning. But no Reverend Bosanquet, and no letters from Humphrey. Dora enjoyed herself greatly playing hymns, and even experimented with the pedals.

She went the following Thursday at the appointed time, and found the situation exactly the same. She went the next, and the next: the same. Music by Bach and Handel and Sir Hubert Parry was left on the music stand, presumably for her use. But no Bosanquets.

'I will not have such literature in my house! Do you hear me!'

'Arnold, Arnold, you will wake Edwin!'

'Will you destroy it, or shall I? But first you will kindly tell me where you acquired it!'

The drawing-room door was open. Dora could even hear Father's breathing, violent and fast. She did not dare, shivering in her nightdress, move further than the top of the stairs. She was consumed with curiosity. Just what had Richard been reading?

'Mr Lofthouse sent for it for me.'

'Lofthouse! Of course, of course. You have not the initiative to get it yourself, but must be fed such iniquitous rubbish by that man.'

'Arnold!'

'Mr Lofthouse is a member of the No-Conscription Fellowship. I have not yet joined, though I am considering it.' Richard's voice, too, was breathy.

Father rustled a paper and began to read. '"*The Tribunal*. Our object . . . the mass of scandalous administration" – do you hear that, Winifred? Scandalous, the work that I do, week after week, from motives of pure patriotism! "Our Point of View: the administration of the Military Service Act must be at once challenged." Price one ha'penny! Can you afford it, may I ask, when you are being supported in this house solely by *my* charity?'

'Father. . . .' Richard seemed to have snatched the paper. 'Listen. This is what happened at one man's tribunal. "It is against Christ's command to fight," he said. What did the Military Representative reply? "Insane views!" If I am to face this sort of thing, Father, I must go prepared!'

'But Richard, they are evil, these Germans!'

'The boy will not listen to argument, Winifred. Do not waste your time on him. One more question I will ask you, Richard.' Dora waited, wondering what it would be. She was becoming quite familiar with the weapons that each side used in this particular battle. Father said, 'How long can you go on saying "I am right" when the whole body of the English nation tells you, in words, in action and by force of law, that you are wrong?'

There is no answer to that one, thought Dora. And for once, Richard agreed with her. 'I don't know, Father. I shall just go on as long as I can.'

Then Richard's footsteps, lighter than Father's but heavier than Mother's, came towards the stairs and Dora scuttled back to her room. But she peeped out again when Richard had gone into his bedroom, and seeing his door ajar she tiptoed across.

'Heyho! You got a rocket!' It was what they used to say, giggling, when they were young.

But Richard, sitting on the bed, looked up at her in dreadful seriousness. She thought she wanted to hit him for being so perpetually earnest.

'Yes,' he said.

Then suddenly she felt as though she wanted to run over and give him a hug – which she didn't, though she did say quickly, 'I wouldn't let it worry you,' before blushing and hurrying back across the landing. She couldn't think why she felt like that until later when, tossing and turning and trying to get to sleep, she remembered how she had felt when the Reverend Bosanquet surprised her at the organ. She had felt embarrassed and guilty – had wanted to *die* of embarrassment and guilt – but she had known that she was right. Richard, sitting there dejectedly on the bed, must have felt like that too, she supposed sleepily. But he must be frightened as well. . . . Prison? Really? Surely a *Fishwick* could never go to prison?

The next morning, at breakfast, there was a letter on

Richard's plate. The name and address on the envelope were typewritten. Richard saw it the instant he came into the room. He took it and put it into his pocket straight away without reading it, and then sat down. Dora saw that the envelope had some kind of official crest on the back.

Father and Mother must have seen the letter, but they made no mention of it. Breakfast was eaten in silence.

'I have a letter for you, Dora.'

Dora was handing back the brown paper bag containing the *Girl's Own Paper* and nearly dropped it.

'I suppose that the person who sent it did not know your home address.' Miss Gossage calmly took the book, handed over the letter, and went to sit behind her desk. 'Venezuela,' she announced. 'Do sit down, Dora. Venezuela. Capital, Dora?'

Dora managed to survive Venezuela, but simply had to go to the lavatory during Brazil. Miss Gossage impassively gave permission. Dora secreted the letter down the front of her dress.

Miss Gossage's lavatory had beautiful wedgwood-blue flowers and scrolls and cherubs all over the bowl. The seat was capacious, a dark brown wood, almost warm to the touch. It was the ideal place to open a mysterious letter from a stranger. She sat down, and tore it open.

It was from Alfred Bosanquet.

She was surprised to find that she had almost forgotten his existence. But now, as she read his small neat handwriting, he rose before her, pale and smiling nervously.

His school was one she had not heard of, but the address was somewhere in Lincolnshire. Flat, desolate, exposed, she thought.

'Dear Miss Fishwick,' he wrote carefully. 'Spring is here and I have seen some early daffodils. How their nodding heads do lift the heart. Have you read the poetry of William Wordsworth? You may borrow my volume of his complete works if it would interest you.

'I am continuing my lessons at the organ. It was fortunate that I was able to discuss it with you. The Easter holidays begin on 29 March.

'I have no news of my brother. My father writes occasionally and sends me tuck. My mother is not well.

'I hope this letter does not offend you. I may have difficulty in posting it but am hoping my friend the cook will take it to the village for me.

'Your sincere friend, Alfred Bosanquet.'

She could see him, writing secretly, attempting an opening – perhaps 'Dear Miss Fishwick, it was so delightful to . . .' – and then screwing it up and throwing it away, eventually lighting on a neutral start, then unable to resist referring to their one vital meeting, and then – oh, how transparent were the workings of his mind! – mentioning the start of the Easter holidays.

This was clearly nothing less than an assignation. However unattractive Dora found him, she could not remain unexcited by the prospect of meeting again, in the dark secrecy of a holy and forbidden place, a young man who so clearly adored her.

But he had no news of Humphrey! And what of the Reverend Bosanquet? He knew of her previous meeting with Alfred, and might be in the church at any time. The thought of going into the church and finding there both Alfred *and* his father, the one wishing to sit beside her on the organ bench and the other to sit in the vestry discussing Humphrey, thrilled and appalled her. Alfred's letter began to tremble in her hand.

She jumped up, remembering that she ought to be drawing Brazil and Venezuela on to the continent of South America. It struck her that she had better not want to go to the lavatory again that morning, or Miss Gossage's tolerance might be stretched too far. She lifted her skirts and did what was necessary, and then ran back to the schoolroom, praying that no questions would be asked. She fixed Alfred's letter again firmly in the front of her dress.

As her pen inscribed the river Amazon down its appropriate curves, her mind went back to the *Girl's Own Paper*'s advice to girls who were in receipt of a letter from a young man. Sandwiched in between information to Disappointed ('the loss of your canary's voice may be only temporary') and comforting words to Lonely Lassie ('endure your isolation by drawing near to Him who is closer than a brother'), there tended to come cautionary phrases directed towards A True Heart or A Perplexed One, indicating that a parent's permission should be gained before venturing to reply to the young man. But poor Alfred: he was so lonely. 'My friend the cook' spoke volumes on his loneliness. There would be no *Stalky and Co* cavortings for Alfred. Should she not take pity on him?

And if she were discovered, and declared to be defiant and outrageous – what then? She did not care. In fact, the prospect of being declared outrageous gave her an inward, warm, suffusing smile.

Seven

DORA'S BEDROOM was at the back of the house, but even so she had no difficulty in hearing it.

'Send out the Army and the Na – vee, Send out the Rank and File. . . .'

She lay in bed, feeling puzzled, reminded of carol-singers. The singing was more raucous, but not untuneful.

'. . . brave old Territorials, They'll face danger with a smile!'

It must be nearly ten o'clock, and she was supposed to be asleep. Might she put on her dressing-gown and go down to ask what was happening? There were no voices in the hall, no doors opening and shutting downstairs. Was one one else curious but her?

She was already out on the landing when she heard the last rousing lines of the song. '. . . to set old England free – Send out my brother, my sister and my mother But for Gawd's sake *don't send me*!' She stopped in her tracks, and at last the meaning of it flooded over her.

Father and Mother must be sitting frozen in their drawing-room chairs. There was no light in Richard's bedroom: he must be sitting there too.

What would Father do? Go out and harangue the ruffians? Arrest them for disturbing the peace? Or might Richard go to them, as a lamb to the slaughter?

But there was total silence.

Then, 'Poltroon!' someone shouted, and it was taken up by the rest. 'Poltroon! Coward! Dog! Worm, worm, worm!'

There was another lull, and then, 'Show us your white feathers! Where are they, then? Bring out your white feathers!'

It was when Dora heard the sound of a pebble against the glass in the front door that she began to be really frightened. She wanted to run back to her room, but she dared not move: it was stupid of her, she should run, she should hide, what if they came crashing in, she would have no defence again them, it would be like Fanny's ravishing German.

At this point Father came out of the drawing-room and approached the front door. Dora held her breath. She could not see Father, however she contorted herself at the banisters, so she closed her eyes. She heard more footsteps between the drawing-room and the front door. Richard was coming out too. There was a pause.

Father opened the front door and said quietly, 'Richard?'

Richard, a tremor in his voice, called out, 'Who is it? Who is it?' Then, more firmly, 'Will you come in and talk about it?'

Dora felt the cold night air on her face and toes. She had forgotten her slippers.

She heard a shout of 'Scrimshanker!' – but it was weak and jittery. Then there was the sound of boots walking away, then running. Father said, 'Huh!' and turned and went back to the drawing-room. But Richard stood at the front door until long after the sound of running feet had died away, and he did not actually move until Mother called shakily to him from the drawing-room, 'Be careful not to catch cold, Richard dear!'

When he had gone in and closed the door, Dora could not bear the thought of going back to bed. She was shivering with cold and fear. But she was seized with a kind of huge delight. She hugged herself for warmth, and whispered to herself in amazement, 'So *that* is what it's like to be really, truly afraid! What a feeble, flimsy kind of fear I have felt until now! Fear of Father, fear of being found out, fear of punishment – they are as gossamer, as snow melting before this . . . this fire of paralysing agony!'

She wanted to scream, but realized that it was too late now for that. She sat there, gripping herself as though she were gripping somebody else, for about five minutes (she was sitting opposite the grandfather clock) before she felt ready to move. Then she released herself and went slowly downstairs.

Her knock was answered by a surprised 'Come in!' from Father. She went in cautiously, and saw Father and Richard standing side by side in front of the fire, and Mother in her chair, not leaning back as she usually did, but forward towards the fire, her face taut and white. Father said, 'Oh! Come in, Dora. I thought it might be one of the servants. Did you hear the . . . disturbance?'

'Yes, Father.'

'And you were afraid?'

'Yes, Father.'

Mother held out a hand. 'Oh – Dora. . . .'

'I think I'm all right, Mother.'

'Come beside the fire, child.' Father and Richard parted like the Red Sea, and Dora knelt down in front of the fire. The coals were low but glowing. Father sat down in his chair, and Richard followed suit.

'I'm sorry if those young men distressed you, Dora,' Richard said. He sounded as though his throat were slightly constricted.

'Savages! The constables will be after them!' Mother dabbed her eyes.

Dora wanted to look at Richard, but could not without turning right around. She turned to Father and said, 'Who were they, Father?'

'I recognized only one of them. He was Harry Grimes, I think – the son of Grimes in leather goods. Grimes asked about six months ago if we could take his son on, but having interviewed him I decided against it.'

Richard said, 'I see.'

'I suppose you do see, Richard,' said Father wearily.

'Arnold, do you think they will come again?'

'I doubt it. That type do not usually have much backbone, as their behaviour tonight shows.'

'Thank goodness they did not wake Edwin and Fanny and Lizzie,' said Mother. 'Dora dear, do go back to bed. Now, you won't think about it any more, will you? Don't lie awake or have bad dreams, dear – I couldn't bear you to fret about it.'

Dora realized that her mother was comforting herself as much as anyone else. She stood up and kissed her.

'Richard,' she said as she turned to go. 'Richard, will you. . . .'

But Father interrupted her. 'Don't bother him, child. Go to bed now. Sleep well.'

She was puzzled by his gentleness, and by the odd air of conspiracy which seemed to have sprung up between Father and Richard. But it was clearly useless to ask any more questions. When she got into bed, she fell asleep without any trouble at all.

She had become quite casual about walking up the aisle, popping her head around the vestry door, nodding at the speechless boy who stood beside the bellows like the village idiot beside the pump, and then settling down at the organ to play. This Thursday, however, the boy shuffled his feet and pointed at the pile of Bibles on the small table, on top of which lay a package.

'For me?' she said, and picked it up. It was inscribed 'For the organ student', and peeping inside the large envelope she saw the sheets of Parry's music which last week had been on the organ ready for her to play. Why put them in a special package today?

She said 'Thank you' to the boy, and took the package to the organ. When she was comfortbly settled, she took the music out.

As she did so, there fell on to her knee and on to the pedals two smaller sheets of paper. One was the familiar flimsy grubby paper which would be headed, '2nd Yorks and Lancs., B.E.F. France'. The other, much larger, cleaner and of superior quality, had on it the handwriting she now recognized as that of Humphrey's father.

Humphrey's letter was on her knee. She seized it.

'Dear Father,' she read. 'I must apologize for not writing to you for some time. I have been kept rather busy. I have received a few letters from you, but the mail is rather disjointed just now.' Her eye flicked to the top of the page, where was written the one word 'Trenches'. How extraordinary to have in her hand a letter written in such circumstances! She read on, 'I wonder if you have had snow. If so, they will have been tobogganing on the Green. We have had some snow, and a great deal of rain. I am rather tired. Fritz is strafing us fairly regularly. How is Mother? Please could you send some quinine and some rat poison.' The letter trembled in Dora's hand. 'I have been told of numerous Rapid Cold Cures but would prefer quinine. I would like to write more but it is not possible just now. Your ever loving son, Humphrey.'

She could find no reason for being moved to tears by this letter. He seemed the same calm, stalwart Humphrey, coolly describing unthinkable events with phrases like 'fairly regularly' and 'rather busy'. But the writing blurred in front of her, and she could imagine a huge rat, several huge rats, scrambling over Humphrey's once-smart uniform while he was asleep, and even scurrying over his face and head. Colds, rain, strafing (what kind of fighting was that?), mud, bodies, rats. Of course it was like that. How could she ever have thought otherwise? But it would not be long, surely, before he was back in his billet, bathed, shaved and in newly pressed uniform, tucking into crisp French bread again and thinking of how to keep the morale of his men high. Surely someone of Humphrey's rank would not be kept in such appalling conditions for long. She propped his letter up in front of Parry's music, and bent down for the other letter.

'Dear Miss Fishwick,' it said. 'I trust that your organ studies are progressing satisfactorily. I enclose a recent letter from my son. Perhaps you would be so kind as to put it back in the envelope with the music, and leave it on the vestry table when you have read it. I am kept at the vicarage a great deal at the moment owing to my wife's illness. I remain, yours faithfully, S. H. Bosanquet (rector).' In fact his signature was illegible, but she presumed that was what it said.

She realized suddenly that the organ had been hissing faintly for some time. That poor boy had been pumping away, expecting the organ to pour forth music at any minute. She put the two letters on the bench beside her and started to play.

But her mind was on the Bosanquet family. What illness did Humphrey's mother suffer from, that he could not write to her directly? Was it Humphrey who needed the quinine for his own cold, or did he want to give it to his men? Did Humphrey ever think of Alfred? Did Alfred worry about Humphrey? And why did the Reverend Bosanquet go to such trouble to share his every communication from France with a young Methodist girl who was almost a complete stranger to him?

Dora was in the dining-room practising one of Bach's three-part inventions in the hope that it would improve her organ technique when the door-bell rang unexpectedly. Fanny was still out taking the afternoon air with Edwin, and Dora heard Lizzie padding slowly along to answer it. She stopped playing.

'Reverend – ! Well, I never did!' Lizzie was not good at disguising her feelings. 'I don't know. . . . I'll tell the Mrs!'

Dora sat on the piano stool, taut.

Lizzie went to the drawing-room. 'It's the, well, madam, it's. . . .'

Dora heard Richard say, 'It will be Mr Lofthouse,' and come out into the hall.

Without thinking whether she ought, Dora got off the stool and rushed to the hall. Richard was saying, 'It's very good of you to come, sir,' and shaking Mr Lofthouse's hand. Mrs Fishwick stood diffidently in the drawing-room doorway, looking pink and at a loss as to what to say.

Mr Lofthouse stepped forward. 'Mrs Fishwick.' He shook her limp hand. 'Forgive me for calling like this. I heard about. . . . I felt I should come to see you.' He turned to Dora. 'It is good to see you, Dora,' he said warmly, and took her hand. His hand was plump and his grip was firm. Phoebe sends you her love. She misses you a great deal, you know.' Dora could not miss the note of reproach in his voice. She wanted to say 'It's not my fault!' but could not.

'Well – er – perhaps you could bring us some tea, Lizzie? And take Miss Dora a cup of milk in the dining-room – yes, you will go on with your practice, please, Dora.'

Doors closed, and Dora sat down angrily and made a lot of mistakes in the Bach. She heard Lizzie take in the tea, and it seemed an age before she came to bring Dora her milk.

'What is it, Lizzie? What has he come for? Close the door, do!'

Lizzie leaned heavily against the back of Father's carver. She said, 'Well, they're on about Tuesday night and pebbles and boys and such.'

'Didn't you hear it all, Lizzie? Oh, it was *terrifying*!'

At this moment Fanny and Edwin could be heard returning, and Lizzie went out and signalled them into the dining-room so that Dora could tell them the ghastly events in every dramatic detail.

'Wasn't he *brave*!' breathed Fanny. 'Don't do that, Edwin, you'll rip my apron, there's a boy.'

'Who, brave?' demanded Dora.

'Mr Richard, scaring them off like that! Oh, I wish I'd woke and seen it all!'

'You'd better get that boy his tea, young Fanny,' said Lizzie firmly, 'or he'll not be ready to say goodnight when himself comes in.'

When Fanny and Edwin had gone, Dora said, 'Lizzie, be an absolute angel and go and ask if they want any more rich tea biscuits or something. I can't wait to hear what Phoebe's father has really come about.'

Lizzie came back and said, 'Well, I don't know if you can make it out, Miss Dora, but it seems the Reverend's going somewhere with Mr Richard and they're going on about how your father isn't going to be there and they seem to be very happy about that, I must say, as though it wouldn't suit them at all for your father to be there, though how your mother could say such a thing in front of the Reverend when she knows your Father has took against the Reverend this last while I don't kn. . . .'

'It's the tribunal!' Dora shouted.

'*Ssh*! For pity's sake, Miss Dora.'

'So Father won't be on it after all! Lizzie, did they mention a day? That letter Richard got must have told them the day.'

'Oh yes, I can tell you that, Miss Dora. They talked about the Reverend going with Mr Richard on one particular day, and that was Monday, I'm sure of that, because that was the day your father wouldn't be there, sitting, I think they said, or something. Now if you could explain to me what's going on, Miss Dora, I'd be more than grateful, because all this upset, and turning against the Reverend, it isn't like the Fishwicks as they used to be, but then I don't suppose with this war and all we can expect. . . .'

'Come into the nursery, Lizzie,' said Dora maternally. 'And I'll tell you and Fanny all about it. Then when Monday comes you'll know what all the hustle and bustle is for. Oh, I wonder if . . . but Miss Gossage would never let me off *again*, and Father wouldn't *hear* of. . . . But I'll ask them if I can go, Lizzie! Cross your fingers for me, won't you?'

Eight

DORA AND HER MOTHER took a hansom to the Town Hall. They usually took the motor bus when they went to the Shop to buy Dora new pinafores or boots or Sunday bonnets, but Mother clearly thought that today a hansom was more appropriate. She was wearing her second-best hat, which was wide and black with a trail of not-too-conspicuous flowers on the brim, and she looked very tired and pale. She put her hand over Dora's as they drove. Neither of them spoke.

Outside the Town Hall, men in toppers and boys carrying papers walked up and down the steps purposefully and went with no hesitation in and out of the large doors. One pasty-faced young man with fair hair caught Dora's eye: he went up half the steps, stopped, paused, came down again and stood, as if waiting for someone but almost certain that they would not come. Near him stood an old man in a flat cap, whose chin was long and nose beaky. He was shuffling his feet in a state of gripping indecision.

Just as Mrs Fishwick turned from paying the cabbie, Dora saw her Father and Richard coming out through the Town Hall doors. The commissionaire was nodding respectfully to Father, and Richard had his head down. A gust of wind blew just as they were at the top of the steps, and Father had to hold his hat on.

'Arnold.'

'My dear, it seems that Richard will not be heard for an hour or two yet.' His voice was comforting, and he seemed calm. 'Perhaps we could go to Sadler's and refresh ourselves?'

Dora was delighted. She had only been to Sadler's twice before, once with all the family to celebrate Richard's first day at the Shop, and once with her mother on the first day they had felt able to leave Edwin alone with Fanny.

She watched the people they passed as they walked along the street. The variety of hats, on both gentlemen and ladies, was astonishing – they certainly did not all come from Fishwick's – and so was the variety of moustaches on the gentlemen. Richard had grown a small gingerish moustache, which he tended to stroke with his finger when he was nervous. At the moment he was striding along beside her in apparent confidence. She wondered what was going on in his mind.

Then from behind them came an unmistakably cheerful voice. 'Richard! Ah, Mr and Mrs Fishwick, I was just. . . .'

'Lofthouse!'

Dora had wondered when Mr Lofthouse would appear. She wished her father would not address him like that. It made him sound like a tradesman. She remembered that Richard had told her once that Mr Lofthouse's father had actually been a tradesman.

'You are not going towards the Town Hall?' He was shaking all their hands.

Father explained about the delay, and Sadler's. He asked, with extreme politeness, if Mr Lofthouse would care to join them at coffee. Mr Lofthouse hesitated, and then said that he would find great interest in hearing the other cases coming before the tribunal. Mother looked relieved, and they parted with strained smiles.

Dora, comfortably seated in a red velvet-covered upright chair, chose a cream doughnut to eat with her coffee.

'You'll get fat,' said Richard.

'Don't tease, Richard,' said Mother. 'Why not have one too? It would sustain you in. . . . It would sustain you.'

'No, thank you, Mother.'

Dora was the only one eating, but she did not mind.

'You will be sixteen, Dora, in a week's time,' Father said in a grave tone. 'A little nearer to the age of discretion, perhaps?' He managed to smile.

Mother said quickly, 'We wondered – Arnold, dear, may I tell her now? It would be so nice to do something happy today as well – Dora, we wondered if, perhaps, a bicycle might be a suitable, well, whether you might like one, for riding on Saturdays, perhaps, or even to school if the weather is not too uncertain?'

Dora almost choked on her doughnut, and a bit of cream got stuck on her chin. She wiped it off carefully, and then said, 'I – oh, Mother, Father! Really? *May* I have a bicycle?'

Father smiled, easily this time, and said, 'We thought it would be appropriate for you now, Dora. I have made enquiries and think that one will be available within the week. Now, drink up your coffee. Richard is beginning to look impatient. It would not give a favourable impression if he were late.'

They walked back, trying not to be seen to hurry, and found that Mr Lofthouse had been in the public gallery and had come down to the foyer to meet them.

'Some of your, er, severer colleagues are sitting today, I fear. Richard, you may be given something of a grilling. Be prepared. I will be ready to witness when required.'

Father took off his hat, brushed some dust off it with his hand and said, turning slightly away from Mr Lofthouse, 'I do not think Richard is one to be intimidated.' It was almost as if the two men were competing to protect and support Richard.

After a few words with the commissionaire, Richard went towards a door on the ground floor, and Father indicated that they and Mr Lofthouse should go up to the public gallery. The wide stone steps curved round and then narrowed towards the top. On the landing the commissionaire nodded to Father as the other had done at the door. They filed in: Mother first, then Dora, then Father, and Mr Lofthouse last.

When Dora had sat down and arranged her skirts, she looked around. Down below them was the council chamber, which was enormous and arranged with curving wooden benches. Sitting at the back at a slightly raised table were five men aged between fifty and seventy, with pens in their hands and paper and ink in front of them. She did not recognize four of them, but the one on the right was a clergyman, and she saw at once that it was the Reverend Stephen Bosanquet.

Despite the daylight which came in through the tall thin windows in three of the four walls, the huge room was lit with gaslamps, and Dora could see that in the middle of his thick grey hair the Reverend Bosanquet had a distinct bald patch. He had been looking up at the public gallery when they came in, but on the instant that he saw her – and she was certain that he did – his eyes flicked down to his paper.

She felt hot under her frock, and her knees trembled beneath her skirts. 'I am full of fear and foreboding,' she thought alliteratively, 'for my brother in his confrontation with this man.' Was this what Mr Lofthouse had meant by Father's 'severer colleagues'? And what of the other four men?

One of them must surely be a retired soldier. He was in mufti, but he sat upright, shoulders square, hair and moustache groomed, hands flat on the table, unmoving. Six medals were pinned on his suit jacket, neat as guards in a line. Of the other three, all looked like officials or businessmen of some kind, but one wore a suit of poorer quality than the others and seemed less at ease. Dora wondered if he perhaps worked in some clerical position in an insurance office or on the railway.

Standing beside the table was a man in the uniform of a senior officer. He had laid his hat on the edge of the table and was at present questioning the man whose case was now before the tribunal.

This man, Dora saw, was the fair young man with the pasty face whom she had earlier seen outside. Now his face was flushed, and he ran his fingers through his hair more often than was necessary.

'Your motives are politics, then, pure and simple!' the officer was saying angrily.

The young man fumbled in his pocket. 'I am a Socialist if that is what you mean, sir. But I can quote from *The Times* to support my case.' He brought out a small scrap of newspaper and screwed his eyes up to read it. 'It says, "The essence of freedom, as we know it and value it, is that the individuals of a nation shall be able to think what they believe to be true and do what they believe to be right." That is from *The Times* of 21 Novem. . . .'

'Do not quote newspapers to us,' interrupted one of the businessmen wearily. He spoke as if he had already heard more arguments that morning than he could take. 'Your conscience surely does not depend on what you read in *The Times*. Have you any religion?'

'I do not belong to any church.'

'Do you love your country?'

'I love the people of my country, and the people of every other country in the world.' He spoke defiantly. Dora thought he would have impressed the five men more by being humble.

'So you love the Germans, who have butchered the womenfolk of Belgium and are threatening to do the same to our wives and children on these very shores?' shouted the man who looked like a railway clerk.

The young man began, 'The people of Germany are not. . . .'

But the five men had been conferring among themselves and now the man in the centre of the table spoke. He looked the oldest of them, but was tall and thin and seemed in vigorous good health.

'We have heard your case, Mr Forbes,' he said decisively. 'Our Military Representative considers that you are a young man of considerable intelligence who has argued himself into a certain nonsensical frame of mind. You have a good physique and would make a fine soldier. Application disallowed.'

Dora looked at the young man. His face had flushed a deeper colour, and his hands were in tight fists. She thought he was going to say something, but then he turned quickly and almost ran towards the door. He ignored the commissionaire and went out, slamming the door violently behind him.

She felt Mother and Father stir beside her, and settle themselves again. Their party was by no means the only one in the public gallery. There was a group of rather oddly dressed people just in front of them, including a man with no hat on and a woman in a dress of lower cut than a Fishwick would consider proper. To their right was a middle-aged pair, one of whom was reading a small Bible, and, behind them, several people of assorted ages sitting very quietly watching every move in the room below. Dora thought that the oddly dressed group might be from a strange political party, and the Bible-reading pair perhaps were Quakers or Christadelphians or some other group that she had heard her father call 'resolute pacifists'.

The next man to appear was an accountant in his mid-thirties. He put forward the case that he should be exempt on grounds of employment, because he ran his business single-handed. Both the Military Representative and the tall thin chairman agreed that the country was in need of expert accountants even in time of war, and it did not take very long for the tribunal to be convinced that his business would collapse if he were recruited. Dora noticed that the Reverend Bosanquet was taking little part in the proceedings, perhaps because the voluble railway clerk was sitting between him and the other members of the tribual and constantly leaned forward bulkily to address the applicant or consult his colleagues.

She was puzzled at the lack of a dock that she had always imagined to be a feature of such proceedings. Then she remembered that her father had told Richard, 'The tribunal is not a court of law, Richard. All you must do is to put your case – such as it is – clearly and without hesitation.' Father had in fact been unusually helpful to Richard in the last few days.

There was a pause before the next applicant came in, and Dora wondered if it would be Richard. She saw Mr Lofthouse cross and uncross his legs.

It was not Richard. It was the old man with the beaky nose and chin. He came in quickly, shuffling as before, and said, without being prompted, 'It's like this, your honour, if my son goes, it's no good, my tailoring, and it's been in the family for three generations, it'll just close down. My eyes and the wife's are failing, you see, and the son's the only one who. . . .' He mumbled on for some minutes before the chairman, kind and firm interrupted him.

As the door opened to let the old man out, Dora could see Richard waiting to come in.

The clock on the wall behind the five men said twenty minutes to one. Richard's must surely be the last case before lunch. It was very stuffy. Dora, in her serviceable wool coat, was very hot but dared not even unbutton it. She stared in front of her, praying that she would not start to feel faint.

Richard had to give his name twice, because on the first occasion his voice was muffled by his hand on his moustache. When he said Fishwick for the second time all the members of the tribunal except the rector shifted and stared at Richard closely. But when the business of his name was over, Richard seemed to gain courage, and he looked directly at the men at the table.

'And the grounds of your application are that you have a conscientious objection to military service?' asked the clerk, formally.

'Yes.'

The lean, vigorous chairman said almost casually,

'Your reasons for this?'

'I consider war to be against the commands of God.'

'How long have you held this view?' The same indifferent tone.

'Ever since I began to hold independent opinions, sir.'

'Hm. Since you are only eighteen, that might not be a very long time.'

The Reverend Bosanquet had been leaning forward during this exchange. Now he spoke, in the sharp bark which was familiar to Dora. 'What Scriptural evidence is there? Tell me that! Quote the word of God against this war!'

This sudden thrust took Richard aback. 'Er – the Sermon on the Mount, sir. "Ye have heard that it hath been said in former times, Love thy neighbour and hate thine enemy. But I say unto you. . . ." '

'Yes, yes, Matthew 5, 43. We have heard the Sermon on the Mount quoted to us every day since these tribunals began.' The rector drew himself up angrily, and his burly neighbour leaned back as if to lend him more of the stage. 'Have you not read Numbers chapter 32, verse 6: "Shall your brethren go to war, and shall ye sit here?" ' Richard opened his mouth and shut it again. 'How can you see your countrymen, your childhood friends, young men of high courage and patriotic spirit, men with their futures bright before them . . . how can you see them, fighting the enemy, shedding their life's blood, paying the supreme sacrifice to protect you and your mother and your father and your sister . . .' Dora's eyes flicked from the Reverend Bosanquet to Richard, and she saw him glance briefly in panic up towards the gallery . . . 'while you stay here in comfort pleading a tender conscience?'

'Could I ask. . . .'

But the sermon was not to be interrupted. 'Have you not read the words, "Vengeance is mine, saith the Lord"? The man who would not defend the womenfolk of his country is a coward and a cad. Tell me this, Master, er, Mr Fishwick: this conscience of yours – is it not, in truth, sheer *funk*?'

Dora heard Mr Lofthouse let out his breath sharply. There was a slight rustle around the chamber, as if in surprise and awe at such oratory. Dora looked quickly at Father. He was frowning deeply, as she had seen him when in pain with his foot.

'You wish to call a witness?' the clerk was saying. Mr Lofthouse got up and went out hastily, nearly tripping over an elderly lady who had just come in.

There was a pause while Mr Lofthouse's appearance in the chamber was awaited. The rector remained leaning forward, face flushed. Two of the other men tapped their pens. The Military Representative took a few steps to the right, and then took a few steps to the left again.

The clerk said, 'You are the Reverend Raymond Lofthouse, minister of the United Methodist Chapel, Hammerton Square?'

'I am.' Mr Lofthouse's brow was puckered, but he looked as though he were trying to return his features to their customary cheerfulness. He said that he had known Mr Richard Fishwick for six years, considered him to be a serious-minded and deeply religious young man. . . .

Dora's head throbbed and she began to feel sick. She closed her eyes.

'Your own opinion of this war is precisely what, Mr Lofthouse?' The bark was unmistakeable. Dora opened her eyes. Her nausea worstened.

By now Mr Lofthouse's features were in their pulpit position. 'I agree with Dr Alfred Salter, the eminent Quaker, who said, and I quote, "Christ in khaki, thrusting his bayonet into a German workman – the Man of Sorrows in a cavalry charge – No! it is impossible – and *we all know it*!" '

Dora made her body go rigid, as she had done by the drawing-room fire, and clenched her fists. Let me see it through, she prayed – let me see it through. She dared not close her eyes again in case she was overcome by dizziness. But the sight of the two clergymen in confrontation sent her stomach into a state of spasm.

The Reverend Bosanquet was impervious to Mr Lofthouse's passion. He said, 'The question before us is this, Mr Lofthouse: is Master Fishwick *for* the national effort or is he against it? Does he demean the sacrifice of others, or does he honour it? Is he to be allowed to put his notion of peace before the redemption of the slave and the deliverance of the tortured?'

In the instant before she fainted, Dora wondered where she would fall. She hoped it would not be on to the back of the wooden bench in front of her. Then she was flooded with nausea, and everything went black.

Nine

THE THING THAT irritated Dora most about her collapse was the fact that she had not been conscious to see the commotion it had caused. She had missed the shocked concern of the crowd, she had missed the expression on the rector's face, she had even missed the actual judgement of the tribunal.

When she recovered, she found that she was lying on a rug in the Town Hall foyer. The first face she saw was not one of her family but the tribunal's Military Representative. She learned afterwards that this masterful and chivalrous man had run out of the council chamber and up to the public gallery so that he, the expert in military casualties, could personally carry her downstairs.

When she opened her eyes he was ordering the crowd of onlookers to move back. 'Air – that is what the patient needs. Ladies and gentlemen, would you kindly give the young lady more air.'

Dora might have enjoyed being the object of so many people's fascinated gaze if she had not still felt so very sick. She closed her eyes again.

'Dora, can you hear me?' Her mother's voice came nearer. 'She is so pale, Arnold. Where is Richard?' Dora felt her hand being taken, and opened her eyes again.

Richard came into view. Dora tried to sit up. 'Richard, what happened? What did they . . . ?'

The Military Representative laid a hand on her shoulder. 'Do not concern yourself with that now, my dear child.'

She lay back and thought, 'Perhaps they acquitted him.' She found it impossible not to think of Richard as being on trial. 'And it was because of me. The rector, horrified at my illness, took Richard's part and argued for his exemption.'

The murmur of voices went on around her. Mother and Father were debating the best way of getting her home; Richard was saying how hot it had been in there; the Military Representative was arranging a glass of water. Cushions were brought – the Lord Mayor's personal cushions? – and she was propped up while she took a sip of water. The coolness slid down her throat. Gradually her head began to clear, and the nausea faded.

Out of the corner of her eye she saw Mr Lofthouse standing over by the main doors. His shoulders drooped, his round face sagged. She could not see the rector anywhere.

Father approached. He asked, matter-of-factly, 'Are you well enough to sit on a chair, Dora?' She said faintly that she thought she was, and Father and the Military Representative helped her over to a small upright chair in an alcove between two tall pillars. She had just sat down when there was a stir among the people still remaining in the foyer, and the members of the tribunal came into view.

Father clearly knew them well. He stood between them and Dora, and she heard him explaining that his daughter had been overcome by the heat of the room.

'A distressing occasion for you all.' This was the chairman. 'I am only sorry that we had to, er. . . . She is recovering, I hope?' He stepped to one side of Father and Dora saw his thin face smiling awkwardly at her. 'On the mend, eh? Stuffy, very stuffy, in there. A bit of fresh air, a bit of lunch . . . right as rain, you can be certain.' He turned. 'Well, gentlemen, it seems the young lady is in good hands. We must refresh ourselves before this afternoon's labours begin. You'll join us, Major?'

The Military Representative shook Father's hand formally and then Dora's. 'Good wishes for your speedy recovery, Miss Fishwick.' Dora said, 'Thank you very much, sir' and smiled weakly. As she did so, she caught a brief glimpse of the rector. He was standing among the other tribunal members, and she thought he had been trying to look at her without being seen. His face looked darker than ever, but she could not tell whether it was from anger or from embarrassment. He seemed to be unaware that the burly railway clerk was speaking to him. Then she saw him jerk his head towards the other man and snap out: 'Humphrey? Due for leave shortly. This month or next. And your boy?'

Dora spent a strange day in bed on Tuesday. Mother sat beside her for five minutes in every hour looking puzzled, Richard put his pale face around the door every so often to say 'All right, then?' and Lizzie brought frequent cups of hot sweet tea. She spent most of the day trying to write her diary. Mother, tearful, said, 'Well, at least you have something to write in it today, dear.'

In fact, she had great difficulty writing. Her brain was so crowded with feelings and impressions that she did not know where to begin.

That evening she was allowed down to dinner. She suspected that Mother and Father did not want another formal meal alone with Richard, and her presence was required to relieve the tension.

Brightly, she said, 'Wasn't Mr Lofthouse marvellous?' Everyone went on with their soup. 'I mean – it was brave of him – whatever his ideas. . . .'

The silence continued. She could not understand it.

Richard laid down his spoon. 'Father considers that Mr Lofthouse's intervention in fact swayed the tribunal towards severity.'

'But. . . .' Dora was confused. How could Father, the most consistent of men, be so contrary? If he could stand by Richard despite their difference of views, why was he not grateful for Mr Lofthouse's ardent support? 'But I thought. . . .' What she had thought was that if Mr Lofthouse was back in favour, so might all the Lofthouse family, and she would be able to renew her friendship with Phoebe. To be able to talk to Phoebe again about life – about the war, about whether scrimshankers were always yellow, about fathers and brothers and fainting attacks. . . .

She saw Father and Mother look at each other quickly across the table. Father's spoon was shaking. Mother said, 'Dora, dear, please do not talk about Mr Lofthouse in that way. It is he who – do not interrupt me, Richard – your father feels that it is he who has persuaded Richard into this . . . this position.' She took out a handkerchief. 'He has no consideration at all for our standing in the community . . . for your father's position on the tribunal.'

Father said, his voice throaty but firm, 'He has no consideration for the fate of this country if we lose this war, Winifred. And the indignity – to see one clergyman set himself against another like that – it was preposterous, degrading.'

Richard was eating slowly, as if he was not listening. Defend him! thought Dora – defend your champion!

Then Father said abruptly, 'We must consider our position with regard to Sunday attendance at chapel.'

Not go to chapel? It was unthinkable, surely?

'Hunstanby Road Chapel might be feasible, though Cranston's extempore prayer leaves much to be desired.'

Hunstanby Road Chapel rose in Dora's mind, a huge ochre brick building of monumental ugliness.

'I will look into the possibilities of Hunstanby Road. And in the meanwhile, Richard . . .' Richard now looked up at Father, but with resignation rather than defiance . . . 'you are not to visit Mr Lofthouse's manse. I have not forbidden it before because you are a grown man. But now I absolutely forbid it, do you hear? I repeat: on pain of the direst penalties, you are not to visit the manse again. Do you understand?'

'I understand, Father,' said Richard.

Miss Gossage was late. Dora was sitting on the schoolmistress's desk at the front of the room, swinging her legs. All the girls stood round her, except Betsy Fuller, who was absent and presumed to be suffering from catarrh again.

'I was trembling – shaking like an aspen leaf. It was truly terrifying. My own brother, facing a court like a common criminal. And my own father could have been sitting at that bench in judgement on him! But Fortune was with us to that extent. Father was sitting up in the public gallery with my mother and myself. Was he, too, trembling? His strong face looked impassive. . . .'

'And your brother?' Minnie Chapman was eager. 'Richard? How did he look? Pale, nervous? Or upright and courageous?'

Dora thought hard. 'He was brave,' she admitted. 'He stood confidently and looked straight at the five gentlemen sitting there as if he had nothing to fear. "I consider war to be against God's law," he said. Well, one of the gentlemen on the tribunal was a clergyman – the rector from St Dunstan's-on-the-Hill.'

Many of the girls attended the parish church. 'But he's so *fierce*! What did he say?'

' "Vengeance is mine, saith the Lord!" he said. And he looked . . . well, you can imagine how he looked.'

The girls rocked with laughter. 'Oh Dora, that's *just* how he is! Do it again!'

Dora did it again, to please them. '"Vengeance is mine!" And then in came Mr Lofthouse, from our chapel, and you know how he looks – oh, I'm the only one that goes there. Well, he's round and red-faced and cheerful and there was he' – laughter – 'and the rector' – more laughter – 'one face getting blacker and blacker and the other getting redder and redder. . . .'

Suddenly the girls' laughter stopped. A few stray giggles, then silence.

Miss Gossage had come quietly in.

'Go to your seats, girls. Get down, Dora.'

Everyone rustled to their places, awed and guilty.

'I will speak to you before you go home, Dora.' For the first time, Dora felt frightened of Miss Gossage.

They all sat quietly waiting. Miss Gossage had her head down and her hands on her knee, almost as if she were praying. Then she looked up.

'Girls,' she said, 'you will have observed that Betsy Fuller is not with us this morning. Her absence is caused by the fact that a telegram arrived at Dr Fuller's house yesterday. Betsy's brother Julian has been killed in France.'

There was a series of small gasps, and then silence. An uncle, a cousin, a relative of a neighbour – these deaths had impinged on Miss Gossage's pupils, but only lightly. But Betsy they had teased and commiserated with daily, and Dora had seen Julian's genial face often when calling at the doctor's for Mother's tonic or Edwin's brown medicine.

'We will sit still for a few moments,' said Miss Gossage. 'Let us think of Julian Fuller, and pray for his family.'

The rest of the day was wretched for Dora. Through Mental Arithmetic and Drake's Voyages and the Wonders of the Ancient World, two pictures kept floating before her: the first was of a Dora-less classroom, and Miss Gossage entering and saying, 'Girls, Dora Fishwick's brother Richard has been killed in France'; and the second was of Miss Gossage with a different sort of grief on her face, staring at Dora wordlessly until Dora burst into tears.

When all the other girls had gone home, Miss Gossage returned to her desk, sat down, and motioned Dora over to her. Her expression was almost as painful as Dora had imagined that it would be. But she could see that Miss Gossage was very angry.

'I hear that you suffered another of your fainting attacks, Dora.'

'Yes, Miss Gossage.'

'But it did not prevent you observing every detail of the scene in the council chamber.'

'I. . . .'

'And using it to gain prestige among your friends. Dora, to practise the art of an actress – for which, I concede, you have more talent than you have for Mental Arithmetic – is not the purpose for which you attend this school.'

Dora was silent. She could not look at Miss Gossage.

'Personally I found your performance wholly abhorrent. In the first place you ignored the fact that the convictions of the two clergymen you were impersonating are convictions on which the moral and spiritual fate of this country will surely hang. Second, and to my mind even more important, you reduced to the level of the music hall the courageous stand of one young man, your brother, for the cause of peace and brotherly love and against the forces of militarism and national pride.'

Dora was paralysed by deep shame. She felt not so much reprimanded as stripped naked. It was true, it was true: she had seen Richard's ordeal only through the confusion of her own petty conflicts. She had seen the whole battlefield of France and Flanders as a mere tug-of-war between Fishwicks, with half-understood clergymen pulling ignominiously on either side. She had supposed that her peculiar friendship with the rector could sway his opinion on conscription; she had seen Mr Lofthouse's heartfelt appeal simply as the return of her key to friendship with Phoebe. And as for Humphrey. . . . 'Miss Gossage?'

'Yes?'

'You said Richard's stand was courageous.' Dora suddenly made a connection. 'But you must know all about exemption, about people having a conscientious objection to military service and all that sort of thing!'

'Yes, I do.'

'But, Julian Fuller . . . Was *he* courageous? Did he die for a cause that is righteous?'

'Those two questions are not necessarily related ones, Dora.'

Dora fought back tears. 'Poor Betsy. I will try to be

kinder to her, really, Miss Gossage.'

'There is something else I think you can do, Dora.'

'Oh, what, Miss Gossage? I was just thinking, if Richard had gone, then I would be feeling just as Betsy is now.'

'No, I don't mean to help Betsy. I mean, to avoid any further confusion or disturbance in your own family. I think you should resist any further temptation to visit St Dunstan's-on-the-Hill.' Miss Gossage was looking straight at her. 'The differences between that church and your family are too great to be bridged by you at the moment, Dora. Perhaps you could confine your spiritual exploration to other branches of the Methodist Church, or, if you must venture farther afield, to the Baptists or the Quakers or the Seventh Day Adventists.'

Dora left, crestfallen. Her moment of revelation was past. She was trapped between Richard, Father and Miss Gossage, and she had somehow to learn to go on living without Phoebe, without Alfred, and without Humphrey Bosanquet.

Ten

DORA'S BIRTHDAY fell on the following Saturday. She woke early and forced herself to suffer by lying in bed until the rest of house was stirring. Then she rose, dressed carefully, and went downstairs.

Father, in the hall, was saying. 'The postboy is late this morning.'

Mother replied with a smile in her voice. 'I doubt if the postboy will be Dora's first consideration on this particular day.'

Dora turned the corner of the stairs and saw, leaning against the wall to the left of the drawing-room door, her bicycle.

'Oh!' Elegant entrance abandoned, she nearly tripped as she rushed the rest of the way down the stairs. 'Oh! Look! Isn't it *beautiful*!'

'For a heap of rubber and iron,' remarked Lizzie, coming through with the porridge-bowls, 'I suppose you could say that it is.'

'It is a machine of the highest quality, Dora.' She could hear the pleasure in Father's voice. 'I hope you will take due care of it. See – the saddle (not seat, mark you, saddle) can be raised or lowered to the height most convenient to you. The chain, here, has a guard to protect your skirts, and should be oiled regularly. Richard will see to that when he does his own. The brakes, here, require careful handling.'

'Don't some ladies wear special bloomers, almost like breeches, when they go bicycling in London?'

'Dora!' said Mother, shocked. 'How very unfeminine of you even to mention it. What things go on in London – one can scarcely imagine.'

Dora laughed. 'I shall feel very daring just riding my bicycle, whatever I'm wearing. I mean. . . .'

'Dora,' said Father, 'I think you have forgotten something.'

'Oh! To say thank you! Oh, thank you, Father, thank you, Mother. It's the most wonderful present I've ever had!'

'No, or rather, apart from that.' He stiffly accepted Dora's enthusiastic kiss. 'You have forgotten that a bicycle requires a certain amount of skill to be ridden with any degree of safety. You must now acquire that skill.'

Richard was coming downstairs. 'I'll teach you, Dora. It looks like a nice spring day outside. Shall we go past the Green and into the lanes after breakfast?'

'Do you think that would be possible, Arnold?'

'I see no reason why Dora's education in the art of bicycling should not begin today. Ah, here is the postboy at last.' He opened the front door. 'A little late this morning, I think, Horace?'

Horace, who stooped and had a lugubrious grin, had been delivering letters to 24 Heathgate for as long as Dora could remember. He must have been well into his thirties, but for some reason he was always known as the postboy. 'It's me mother,' he said, the grin quivering. 'Down with the quinsy again, sir. Third time this winter, sir.'

'Ah well, Horace, spring seems to have come at last. Any letters for the Fishwick family?'

'Well, sir, I said to meself as I come up this path, I said, it must be a birthday of somebody's, I can't think whose, but if I remember rightly it was just about this time last year that the young lady here. . . .'

'Oh, give me them, Horace! How many are there?'

'Now, Dora. There's no need to be hasty.'

'And just one for Mr Richard. And you left out in the cold, sir, with nobody to love you! What a shame. Well, I must be on my way and then back to the poor old lady.'

Mother peered over Dora's shouder. 'Has Great Aunt Marion remembered, dear? She's getting so frail – ah, yes, I recognize her writing. That's from Scarborough; it's a thick one – the Bertram cousins will have sent you a pretty lace handkerchief as usual. And who is this one from, with a local postmark?'

Dora tore it open.

'"With our continuing affection, Phoebe and family,"' read Mother. 'Well! Perhaps it's what they see as Christian forgiveness, but really it seems to me it's only. . . .'

'Was your communication of any particular interest, Richard?' asked Father. But Richard had already turned to go back upstairs.

'Where are you going, Richard dear? Your porridge is on the table!'

'I've forgotten to – er – brush my trousers, Mother. I'll be down in a moment.'

'Your letter, Richard!' Father began again, but Richard was gone. Father and Mother exchanged glances.

Dora sensed that they were frightened rather than angry. 'What do you think Richard's letter was about, Father? Please tell me – I am sixteen now.'

'Not on your birthday, dear,' said Mother shakily.

But Father said, 'She will know about it sooner or later, Winifred. I think that Richard has received his military orders, Dora.'

'You mean he has been called up?'

'That is the generally used term, yes. Now, can we all go and eat our breakfast before it is completely cold?'

'Edwin!' shouted Dora. 'If you put your fingers in the spokes you'll get them chopped off, so! Fanny, stop gawping and take him back into the house.'

She was out of temper with Fanny. In return for a description of what it was like to fall into a swoon, Dora had demanded to know whether a woman's abdomen burst open when she had a baby. Fanny had said it wasn't a fit thing for a girl of her age to be curious about; Dora had said Fanny wasn't telling because she didn't know herself; Fanny had retorted that she knew very well but didn't want to aggravate the mind of a young lady; Dora told her not to use words she didn't know the meaning of and not to be insolent.

Richard, testing his brakes, said, 'I wish you wouldn't talk to Fanny like that, Dora.'

'Oh, don't give me a sermon on my birthday, please. Are we ready to go?'

'I am, if you are. I don't think we'd better mount just yet, though. We'll walk to the top of Millerby Road hill and then turn into the quiet lanes before we start to ride.'

Dora had wondered if Richard would forget, in the circumstances, to buy her a birthday present. But he had remembered: on the breakfast table beside her plate had been a pair of beautiful tan-coloured kid gloves. She was wearing them now; they felt like a second skin. 'Where did you buy these, Richard? Not at the Shop?'

He shook his head and smiled. 'Watch the handlebars as you walk. They'll lead you all over the place if you don't keep your eye on them.'

'But where? Richard! Not at Rubbish and Grumble?' Redditch and Grimble were the hated rival, who just before the war had moved into new premises a hundred yards along the main street from Fishwick's. 'Oh, you lucky pig! I've never even been in there! What's it like?'

'Inferior, of course. Shoddy, low-class goods. But their glove and scarf department. . . . Oh!' He stopped walking, and Dora looked up from her bike and nearly wheeled into him.

'Look what you're. . . . Oh, I see.'

Coming towards them on the other side of the road, striding vigorously, was the tall thin chairman of Richard's tribunal.

Dora thought they were unwise to have stopped. Now they would either have to start walking again, and so seem to be trying to ignore him, or else have to wait until he was level with them, and be forced into conversation.

Richard started walking slowly. When the man was near, Richard called over to him, 'Good morning, sir! Spring in the air, I think?'

The tribunal chairman looked embarrassed. 'Er, yes, yes, good morning to you! Quite recovered, I hope, Miss Fishwick?'

But by the time she had thought of a suitable reply, they were well past him. Richard turned briefly and said, 'As I thought. He's going to see Father.'

'What for?'

'I suppose they'll discuss tactics to get me to change my mind.'

'Tactics?'

'Oh, like telling me I'll be in prison for the rest of my life, or am certain to be shot, or something. They've tried the honour of the country, and the shame on the family.'

'Shot! But, Richard, you might as well go to the trenches and be killed in action, like Julian Fuller! Why have we stopped?' They had just started up the hill towards the church.

He said, 'You just haven't understood me at all, have you, Dora?'

'Well, I know you say it's against God's law, but. . . .'

'But deep in your heart of hearts you think I'm a coward, don't you?'

She blushed, and started walking again, quickly. It was hard work, pushing the bicycle uphill, almost as hard as pushing Edwin in the perambulator. She became aware that they were approaching the church.

'If you think I'm frightened, you're right, in a way.' Richard caught her up. 'I suppose I would be frightened if I were faced with death at the Front. But I would go *if* I thought it right.' There was a hint of hesitation in his voice, as though he hoped that what he said was true. 'But I am absolutely certain that it is wrong. That's why I stick to my guns, even though I am frightened. Yes, I'm frightened of being arrested, being taken to a barracks and made to put on uniform, being insulted when I refuse. . . .'

'Is that what will happen?'

They stood, puffed, at the top of the hill. Dora wondered what she would say if Alfred or Humphrey were suddenly to appear.

Richard took out of his pocket a small pamphlet.

'What's that?' Dora took the pamphlet. ' "The Military Service Act – Fully and Clearly Explained." Another present from Mr Lofthouse?' She opened it. ' "If he still persists in his refusal he will be taken by force and will be liable to all the penalties. . . ." Oh, Richard!'

' "Except that he cannot be put to death," ' Richard completed the sentence. 'No, here, this is the pamphlet I was really looking for. It's from the paper Father was in such a wax about, *The Tribunal*. It says. . . .'

But Dora was in terror of meeting one of the Bosanquets. Perhaps the rector might approach, or even his invalid wife hobble towards them, and find Richard reading her excerpts from *The Tribunal*! 'Come on, Richard, it *is* my birthday – am I going to ride my bicycle or am I not?'

Irritated, Richard folded the newspaper and pamphlet and put them away. But he could not leave the subject. As they walked down the hill with the Green on their left and the Georgian terraces on their right, he said, 'Our old friends the Harmers live in one of those, you know. Number eleven, I think it is. They moved a couple of years ago. I passed Frederick Harmer in the street the other day.'

'How is he? What is he doing now?'

'I haven't any idea. He wouldn't speak to me. He cut me dead.'

Miss Gossage's was now closed for the Easter holidays, and since Richard was not working at the Shop he was able to give Dora cycling lessons every day. It was good to be out in the breeze and sunshine. She was soon aloft, wobbling precariously at first, but then suddenly she gained confidence and was away.

'Hooray!' shouted Richard as she left him behind. She thought he was happier now than she ever remembered. 'Now turn around and come back!'

The lane was very narrow. She rode right over to the left-hand side and then turned the handlebars to the right.

'I meant, get off and turn round!' she heard Richard shout.

She realized, too late, that there wasn't enough space even for an expert cyclist to turn around in. She took fright, pulled the handlebars back again, and steered wildly towards the ditch.

'Dora! What a bore! Are you hurt?'

But she was only shaken, and very dirty. 'It's your fault! Why didn't you *tell* me to get off before I turned?'

'I *am* sorry!'

She got up and tried to brush the dirt off her coat, but her hands were dirtier still. 'Now look what you've done! Father will never let you take me cycling again if Mother tells him you've brought me home in this sort of mess! Oh, you're *hopeless*, Richard, you always have been and you always will be!'

She stopped when she saw the look on his face.

'Do you really think that, Dora?'

'Think that . . . ?'

'I've always been hopeless? And always will be?' Quoted back at her, the words sounded appalling. 'Yes, you do. So does Father. Mother doesn't, but that's hardly important.' He turned away. Dora hadn't the least idea what to say. Any denial now would seem false, and in any case Father's opinion was paramount. Richard must have been thinking along the same lines, because he said, not quite turning to face her, 'So do you *see* why I've got to make a stand against him, now that I know he is wrong and I am right? I *know* it, Dora, I *know* it! And if I give way now, that would be real cowardice. I would lose his respect for ever – for in the last few weeks I have gained a little of it, I'm sure I have.'

Dora thought, You would lose your respect for yourself, too, which was such a surprising thing to have entered her head that she could not quite bring herself to say it. Instead she said, 'Look, isn't this lane the one that leads into Banderbridge Road? And if you go down there far enough you get to Victoria Crescent.'

'The manse!'

'Yes. How long have we been out?'

Richard took out his watch. 'Only three-quarters of an hour.'

'They won't expect us back for another hour, at least. We could cycle down there – will you stay on the outside of me when we're cycling on the road? – and you could see Mr Lofthouse and I could see Phoebe and I could get cleaned up a bit.'

'Dora, you're a wizard – I mean a witch – or something, anyway!' Halfway to laughter, Richard pulled her to her feet. He straightened the bicycle while she wiped her hands on a dock leaf, and then they mounted and pedalled away down the lane.

Eleven

IT WAS STRANGE, visiting the manse in as illicit a way as Dora had visited St Dunstan's-on-the-Hill.

They were welcomed with open arms, literally so in Mrs Lofthouse's case. Mr Lofthouse wrung their hands painfully; Phoebe stood behind shyly. Dora moved away quickly towards her while Richard explained about the bicycle and the fall.

'Dora, my dear girl,' exclaimed Mrs Lofthouse, 'your coat! Give it to me – we'll have it clean in a trice. You must feel quite battered. And hungry too, if I know the Fishwicks. Phoebe darling, take Dora to your bedroom and I'll have Elsie bring up a jug of warm water. Now you two men, sit yourselves down beside the fire, you must have lots to talk about.'

Phoebe and Dora giggled all the way upstairs. Dora couldn't think what they were giggling about, but it was just so good to be with Phoebe again.

'And how is he bearing up?' asked Phoebe excitedly when they were in the bedroom. '*Poor* Richard! That *awful* rector! And they told him he should do non-combatant service! But the Act especially said that absolute exemption could be granted.' Dora had forgotten how marvellously clear-headed Phoebe was. 'And what did your father say? Oh, he must be *terrifying* to live with! I don't know how you *stand* it! Oh, thank you, Elsie – Elsie, did you know Miss Dora fainted right in the middle of Mr Richard's tribunal! And a great big soldier carried her all the way downstairs! You must have written a fantastic diary about it, Dora, honestly. I wish you'd let me read it – no, no, I know it's private.'

'The diary's getting terribly difficult these days, Phoebe. How's yours? It's just that I'm so, well, torn apart. . . .'

They were so long upstairs that Mrs Lofthouse was already handing round sandwiches and sugar cakes when they came down to the living-room. Mrs Lofthouse sat them down and passed them plate after plate; Dora's coat hung over a chair beside the fire. Mr Lofthouse and Richard were talking about Ireland, Dora couldn't think why.

As they drank hot chocolate, Mrs Lofthouse said, 'Well, Dora, and how do you find Mr Cranston of Hunstanby Road?'

'It's difficult to say, Mrs Lofthouse. Mr Cranston is, well . . . and the chapel's so horrible, though it's got a pipe organ, which is lovely.'

'You know about organs, do you? But then of course you've always been musical, haven't you, Dora dear. Phoebe, Dora's plate is empty. Isn't it wonderful to have her back, Phoebe? What you two will get up to I tremble to think. . . .'

'They're not actually supposed to be here, Mother. Isn't it ridiculous? Just think, we've known each other. . . .'

'There's no need to be rude about Mr Fishwick, Phoebe. He's a very upright man, and we must presume that he thinks he's doing the right thing.'

'But it *is* ridiculous, isn't it, Mother, if I can't meet Dora? Oh Dora, you can't think how impossibly dull it's been without you. Mother's lessons are just as lovely, but that Wimbush girl came in your place, and you know how *humble* she is, and polite, and proper. . . .'

'And all the other attributes I've tried to encourage in you, Phoebe dear, so don't be spiteful, please. But Dora, we must make, er, tactful arrangements for you and Richard to come to see us regularly. You say he is giving you cycling lessons?'

'But,' Dora got a word in, 'Father said on pain of the direst penalties. . . .'

'My dear Dora,' said Mrs Lofthouse, entirely serious for a moment, 'Richard is facing the direst penalties in other directions just now, so if he incurs your father's displeasure in the course of gaining support and a guiding hand in those directions, I feel sure he can face it. And I expect you can stand up for yourself too, Dora?'

Dora thought she could. So the three of them put their heads together, and arranged a time convenient to all parties for Phoebe to go out cycling with Dora and for Richard to come again to the manse.

It was all too easy. Mother said continually that Richard must have all possible fresh air and exercise before he was 'called away' and Father, these days, acceded to almost any reasonable request. Dora thought he seemed uncomfortable in Richard's presence. He was dogged, too, by constant pain in his foot. He never mentioned it himself, but Mother murmured regularly that they should consult Dr Fuller, and snatched Edwin away when he tried to clamber on to Father's knee.

Edwin was becoming quite human at last. He talked in proper sentences, and led Fanny the same kind of dance as he used to lead Mother. Dora noticed that he was beginning to talk to Father, to ask him why he didn't cut his eyebrows like he cut his hair, and why you could nearly see your face in his boots. Father gave him a straightforward reply to these questions, which Dora was sure he had never given to herself or Richard.

As for Fanny, Dora had nearly given her up. It was sickening how she doted on Edwin, and she told the same old boring stories about Marie Lloyd and the Crimean War over and over again. In any case, she was practically illiterate; she had never even heard of Rupert Brooke or Thomas Hardy – that Thomas Hardy whom Miss Gossage had tantalizingly mentioned and then said she didn't think she could let Dora read just at the moment.

And Dora had Phoebe back at last. Three times a week they met without fail, except once when a wild April thunderstorm prevented them. It took a little while to regain the old intimacy, but gradually Dora found herself daring to talk frankly.

'. . . and so we sheltered in the church, and *who* do you think was there?'

'A dark and handsome stranger?'

'Well, not exactly. . . .'

Phoebe was intrigued by the Bosanquets. 'Let's free-wheel down Millerby Road hill, then see if we can ride to the top of the church hill without having to get off. Then, when we're puffed, we'll have to sit and rest by the church gate, on that bit of wall.'

'But it's so near *home,* Phoebe. Someone might see us!'

'Scared?'

Sometimes Dora thought that Phoebe should have been born a boy. 'All right, then.'

They couldn't fulfil their plan for nearly a week, for Easter intervened with its interminable chapel attendances for both of them. Dora found that Mr Cranston had a particularly graphic imagination. On Good Friday he described the Crucifixion in every detail, from the thorns pressing bloodily into Christ's pale brow to His final tortured cry of despair. She tried earnestly to picture Christ on a hill outside Jerusalem nineteen hundred years ago, but only succeeded in imagining a pale young man in the trenches with a bullet through his heart. She remembered horrifying tales told by Mrs Lofthouse, who was helping out at the makeshift hospital in the old coaching-inn – tales of British soldiers hung up on German wire like scarecrows, and men light-headed with rum and fatigue staggering over the bodies of their dead comrades before going over the top to be shot to bits themselves. One of those men might be Humphrey.

She wondered during the Good Friday service whether she might faint again, but she thought she probably would not, because she had noticed some regularity in her fainting attacks, and the time had not come round again yet. When would she have the courage to talk to Phoebe about that?

They had arranged to meet at the top of Millerby Road hill at two o'clock on the Thursday afternoon after Easter. It was a windy day, but bright. Richard and Phoebe shook hands with each other politely, and then Richard started to cycle off in the direction of Banderbridge Road.

'Nothing yet?' asked Phoebe as they watched him go.

'Nothing.'

'Isn't he frightened?'

'Honestly, Phoebe, he's . . . well, you've seen him. He's very happy. Once I went into his room to see if he could lend me some blotting-paper and I found him on his knees praying, and it wasn't even bedtime. But apart from that he seems just ordinary.'

'What I can't fathom,' said Phoebe, 'is why he doesn't join the Christadelphians or the Quakers and go and do some hospital work somewhere.'

'He says you can't do a thing like that just because it's convenient.'

'Well, no, but surely hospital work's very worthy? Sometimes I think these conscientious objectors really *want* to be martyrs.'

'You mean like being burnt at the stake, you know you'll get to heaven because of it?'

'Exactly.'

They mounted and freewheeled gently down Millerby Road hill. Then they struggled up beside the Green, and Dora thought of Richard being snubbed by Frederick Harmer. Fancy making everybody hate you, not only your inferiors like Harry Grimes, but your childhood friends and intimates too! She could see the attraction of being a martyr, but she couldn't imagine herself ever going that far.

At the top of the hill Dora glanced towards the church. There was no one in sight.

'Down the hill and back up again!' shouted Phoebe.

The other side was much steeper, and they had to watch their brakes as they went down. Dora had no time to worry about being seen. Then they turned around and pedalled laboriously back up again. Phoebe was way ahead of her. Her legs ached and her lungs felt like bursting. 'I'm *going* to do it, I'm *going* to do it, I'll *not* let Phoebe beat me!' But she was starting to wobble, and just before the top of the hill she half-stepped and half-fell off her bicycle and stood, shaking all over, exhausted.

Phoebe was sitting calmly on the appointed wall, and she was being approached by two young men.

Dora, still red-faced and perspiring, had started to wheel her bicycle towards Phoebe by the time she realized who the two young men were. She wanted to turn and run, but no, Alfred had seen her.

He was even plainer than she remembered, and about an inch smaller than she was. He almost ran towards her.

'Miss Fishwick! How delightful! I return to school next Wednesday, and was so hoping that Fortune would enable us to meet.' He would make a good Jane Austen curate, she thought, suitable for marrying off to somebody's younger sister.

She tried to stop panting, tucked some stray bits of hair back under her bonnet with her free hand, and then shook hands with him. She hoped her hand was not too damp. She could not bear to look beyond him to the other young man.

'I . . . my new bicycle, you see. . . .'

'This hill is simply beastly, isn't it? I think you're so brave to try it. Let me wheel your machine. And you must meet Humphrey. I did tell you about Humphrey, didn't I?'

Dora, relieved of her bicycle, straightened her skirts and tried to breathe deeply. She hardly had time to think 'This is my moment of moments' before a thin hand was approaching hers. She said, 'How do you do?' breathlessly, and looked up.

He had a scanty moustache and was a little taller than Alfred, but was rather like him in appearance, with scarcely more significance in the chin and the same expanse of forehead. They were neither of them in the least like their father, except that Humphrey's hair was straight and stiff and brown where the rector's was straight and stiff and grey. Humphrey's eyes were a pale grey-green, and it struck her immediately that there was only one word to describe the emotion that was in them. It was fear.

His hand, in fact, was trembling. 'Miss, er, Fishwick. Your father's shop . . . many times.' She withdrew her hand, and he said quickly, 'Will you excuse me? I have to see my mother.' Then he turned and walked quickly back through the church gate.

Alfred seemed not in the least inclined to follow his brother. He stood between Dora and Phoebe, shifting from one leg to the other, smiling. Dora recovered herself sufficiently to introduce Phoebe to him.

'Your brother doesn't seem awfully well, if you don't mind my saying so,' said Phoebe.

Alfred stopped smiling. 'He isn't. Oh no, he isn't. Father's terribly worried about him, and Mother is spending all her time in bed.'

'Oh, your mother's not well either?' Phoebe was conversing with complete confidence, and Dora was content to let her. She felt numb.

'She's never well, my mother, never at all. Not since the war began, anyway. Before that she just thought we might get knocked down by a motor car, but now she's sure Humphrey's going to get done for by the Boche.'

'Well, I suppose that's a bit more likel. . . .' Phoebe stopped herself in time. 'Mother says the war's simply dreadful. Men are, well, being sent into battles just because some old officer prefers playing polo to doing his job. And now they're using gas. It's monstrous!'

'Oh!' Alfred seemed taken aback to find Phoebe so different from his adored Miss Fishwick. 'Oh, I don't think the war's like that at all. Humphrey says someone told him it'll be over by August Bank Holiday.'

'Lord Kitchener says it'll go on for another three years,' said Phoebe imperturbably. 'Has your brother got what they call shell shock?'

He looked nervous. 'Of course not. He's not *windy,* if that's what you mean. But three of his men were killed only the day before he came on leave.'

'Poor, poor Humphrey!' burst out Dora.

Alfred turned to her gratefully. 'Yes, Miss Fishwick. We're all trying to back him up in every way we can. He's so courageous. I know I'd throw in the towel if I were in his shoes. Look at this.' He put his hand in his pocket. 'Look, this is the sort of thing that keeps their spirits up.'

He took out a crumpled piece of newspaper and unfolded it. Dora thought for an uncanny moment it might be an issue of *The Tribunal.*

'It's the *Wipers Times.* Wipers – Ypres, you see? A young captain, resourceful fellow – no, not a particular friend of Humphrey's – found an old printing-press in a bombed-out building, and hey presto! What have we here?' He opened up the paper. ' "Agony Column. Will any patriotic person please lend a yacht and £10,000 to a lover of peace. Size of yacht immaterial." ' Alfred swayed as he laughed, and his laughter was infectious. 'And listen to this! It's a poem called "The Ration Carriers". ' He read it, laughing every other line. 'This is the last verse:

"So you chaps back in Blighty
Who haven't got the grit
To go and take the shilling
And to come and do your bit.
Just now and then remember
At night time, ere you sleep,
The men who carry rations
On the road from Pop to Ypres." '

Phoebe looked at Dora, and Dora stopped laughing.

'Oh, Humphrey says he just doesn't know how to talk to us who are sitting at home, warm and comfortable.'

'There are other things to think about,' said Phoebe coldly, 'besides the trenches. What is your opinion, for instance, about this rising in Ireland?'

Alfred clearly hadn't heard of it. 'Ireland? But there's always trouble there. Do listen to this, Miss Fishwick. This is an advertisement: "Wonderful film, *He Didn't Want to Do It,* featuring Wata Funk, The Conscientious Objector." Oh, don't go, Miss Fishwick, Miss – er – Lofthouse!'

Phoebe had taken hold of Dora's hand and was pulling her away.

'Phoebe! Our bicycles!'

They turned back. Dora was blushing.

'Here you are, Miss Fishwick. What a splendid machine it is – shall we meet again?' He held on to it until she replied. 'I hope. . . .'

'If you are returning to school on Wednesday,' said Phoebe, 'it seems unlikely that our paths will cross for some time.'

Alfred flashed a look of pure fury at her. Dora liked him better for that than for anything else she had seen him do.

When they reached the bottom of the hill, they realized they had come the wrong way.

'Phoebe! We've got to meet Richard back at Millerby Road!'

Phoebe braked sharply and got off. 'Providence preserve us! Will we meet *him* again? Dora, how *did* you contrive to involve yourself with such an *oafish* young man?'

'We'll have to go back, anyway.'

One miserable, the other furious, they wheeled their bicycles back up the hill. As they approached the crest, Phoebe hissed, 'He's still there!'

He was standing behind the gate, in the shadow of a yew tree. The two girls mounted hastily, and were too busy concentrating on their bicycle-riding to return his hesitant wave.

As she wearily pedalled up Millerby Road, Dora was almost ready to cry. She and Phoebe did not speak at all.

But as they neared the place where they usually met Richard, she looked up from the handlebars and saw Richard talking to someone.

She nearly fell off her bicycle. 'It's Fanny!' She wobbled the last few yards and dismounted. 'Fanny! Whose bicycle is that? And when did you learn to ride?'

Fanny said, enjoying every word of it, 'Oh, I learned how to ride one of those *years* ago, Miss Dora, when you was about in your cradle. Your mam's neighbour lent me this one for a very special occasion.' She looked significantly at Richard. 'I've been sent to warn Mr Richard. There's a couple of gentlemen wanting him at the house. One of them's a policeman. They say it's urgent, and your mam's crying. I expect they've come to take him away.'

Twelve

THIS IS THE END, thought Dora, as the summer term opened with sun and showers and rainbows. Richard has been taken away, Phoebe is angry with me, Alfred has gone, and Humphrey . . . Humphrey not only was not there in the flesh, he could not even enter her mind without her being suffused with embarrassment and grief. His eyes haunted her, those grey-green eyes below the pale forehead, eyes that had never flashed or sparkled or been uplifted in valour. To be deprived of friendship and adventure – *that* she had grown accustomed to. But to be deprived of the wild yearnings of her imagination – this she could hardly bear.

But Phoebe had not forsaken her. One day shortly after the beginning of term, Dora found her on the way home, lurking in a gateway between Miss Gossage's and Heathgate.

'Surprise!'

'Phoebe! You beast, you made me jump.'

Betsy Fuller, with whom Dora had taken to walking home recently, hovered with interest. Dora said firmly, 'Goodbye, then, Betsy. See you tomorrow. . . .Her brother was killed, isn't it awful?' she muttered under her breath to Phoebe as Betsy walked slowly away. 'You remember Julian Fuller?'

'Yes. And did you know that Mr Bennett died from wounds? He was going to be a lay preacher, Father says. Poor Mrs Bennett, five fatherless boys, just think of it.'

'Oh, I'm so glad to see you, Phoebe. I thought that

meeting with Alfred. . . .'

'Well,' said Phoebe practically, 'I couldn't just desert you, could I, or you'd get even more tied up with nincompoops like that. Anyway, I want to hear if there's any news of Richard.'

'There's nothing yet. Your father would probably hear before we do. Doesn't he get information from that organization he belongs to?'

'He says Richard's probably been taken to Richmond Castle. I can't bear to think about it, honestly, Dora. They might be insulting him, beating him, leaving him naked. . . .'

'They wouldn't!'

'They would, Dora. Father has had letters from men who have been cruelly misused. But others say they've told the soldiers why they're against the war, and the soldiers have agreed with them!'

They walked slowly, eking out the journey.

'How have your parents taken it?' Phoebe asked.

'It's peculiar,' Dora answered. 'Mother seems somehow *content*. She's always doted on Richard, you know. *She* doesn't care if he isn't brainy or successful. She said to me the other day – not when Father was listening, of course – "It's a bit like your uncle Richard Fishwick going off to South Africa. You miss them, you're afraid for them, but somehow you know they're doing the right thing." '

'Really, Dora, what a muddled thinker your mother is! Your uncle Richard went out to South Africa for fame and fortune, whereas *your* Richard. . . .'

'Oh, I know, I know, he's making a stand for peace and love and all that. But Mother means that she can trust Richard to live his own life without being ordered about by her and Father. I only wish they'd start trusting *me* like that.'

'What about your father?'

'He hardly says anything about Richard. Actually, Phoebe, I don't think he's very well. He limps about, and sometimes I see him really wince with pain. But he just won't see the doctor.'

They stopped at the corner of Heathgate. Dora looked down towards the house, which was just out of sight around the corner, and said, 'Fanny's been dreadful, you know, since that day. She keeps on saying "Where would you be, then, Miss Dora, if I was to tell them?" '

'What would they do to you, do you think, if they found out you'd been meeting me?'

'The worst thing is, Phoebe, it isn't only meeting *you*. She knows about Alfred, because she was there that snowy day in the church, and when she was cycling to warn Richard she saw him again where he was standing, in the churchyard.'

'Oh! I can just hear her! "You've been seeing that young man again, Miss Dora, go on, haven't you? I'll tell on you, I will!" '

Dora looked down Heathgate again, as if Fanny might suddenly appear. She leaned towards Phoebe and said in a low voice, 'She's made me promise to ask Mother to give her a rise in wages!'

'But that's blackmail!'

'Is it? I've always wondered what blackmail was.'

'Are you going to?'

'Well. . . .' She hardly dared admit it to Phoebe. 'Well, I said that it was nothing to *her* what I did with my life, but I did think that £15 a year was rather mean, and I would talk it over with Mother if I got the chance.'

'Dora, you. . . .'

'I must go, Phoebe. They'll be wondering where on earth I am. Meet me again, won't you – same place, same time?'

Miss Gossage, too, was concerned about Richard. Every other day she would say, 'Any letter from your brother, Dora?' or 'Have your parents received news yet?' At last Dora was able to tell her what she wanted to know.

'Good. We'll be doing needlework this afternoon. Bring your patchwork up to my desk and you can tell me all about it.'

Dora had worked hard for Miss Gossage's approval this term. She had done a masterly essay on the Rise of Puritanism, had read the part of Cordelia with 'passion and dignity' (those were Miss Gossage's very words) and had stretched herself almost to the limit in being kind to Betsy Fuller. Miss Gossage had lent her *Under the Greenwood Tree* and *Far from the Madding Crowd* by Thomas Hardy. 'If your parents ask any questions,' she said, 'tell them that these books are by the man who wrote the poem "Men Who March Away" for *The Times* in 1914.'

'Now,' she said as they settled to the patchwork, 'tell me about Richard. Won't that clash?' Dora had put a purple patch next to an orange one. 'Beige, yes, that's better. Has he maintained his stand?'

'Maintained . . . ? Yes, oh yes.' Dora realized that Richard's sticking to his guns had not been in doubt in her own mind. 'He's going to go through with it now, I'm sure. He was taken to the barracks, as he expected, and in the, er. . . .'

'Guard room?'

'Yes, in the guard room he was told to put on uniform. Well, he knew this would happen. So he refused. But Miss Gossage, the amazing thing is that the captain was very friendly. He said to Richard, "Now, I can see that you're an educated man. I assure you that it would be in your best interests to obey." I thought he would be abused and beaten, didn't you?'

Miss Gossage sewed thoughtfully. 'Not always, Dora, not always. And what happened then?'

'The captain went away, and another one came back later and tried again. This one was a bit brutal, but Richard didn't say in what way. Then the first man came back and called him a . . . a damned fool, and summoned a corporal. "Watch this!" he said to the corporal. "Private Fishwick, put on that uniform." "No," said Richard. "I must respectfully refuse to obey any military order." So the captain said, "You witnessed that, Corporal?" and told Richard he would, I don't know, have a trial or something in due course.'

'A court martial,' said Miss Gossage. 'Yes. And how has he been treated by the ordinary soldiers?'

'They mock him, call him names – but he's used to that, Miss Gossage. He said one man hit him, but again he didn't say how badly. Then the same captain came, and spoke severely to the man who had hit him, and then said to Richard, "If you want to get a letter out to your family, I'll make sure it reaches them safely." Wasn't that good of him, Miss Gossage?'

'"God moves in a mysterious way," as your father might say, Dora. Had he been court-martialled by the time he wrote the letter?'

'No, it seems not. What will happen next, Miss Gossage? I mean, they can't just go on giving him orders and having him refuse to obey them.'

'They are given small punishments at first, Dora, like being confined to barracks or being put on bread and water. Then, well . . . it all depends whether they remain in this country or are sent to France.'

'If he is sent to France, will they send him to the trenches and make him fight?'

'I doubt if it would go on as long as that.' Miss Gossage turned to another girl who was standing at the desk. 'There, Beryl. Don't pull the thread so hard, no wonder it breaks.' She waited till Beryl had gone to sit down, and then said, 'There are various punishments that are applicable only to the military zone. Those punishments are, of course, the most severe.' Abruptly she asked, 'I hope your parents are in good spirits?'

'Er, yes, reasonably so, I think, Miss Gossage.'

'Good. They will need to be.'

'Miss Gossage?'

'Yes, Dora?'

'I suppose it's through the Quakers that you know all about this sort of thing?'

'Yes. I have several friends who are conscientious

objectors.'

'But I thought all the Quakers were against books, and plays, and music, and all the things you enjoy?'

Miss Gossage laughed. 'Do you know, Dora, *I* thought that all the Methodists were quiet, and well-behaved, and obedient to their parents! It's very confusing, isn't it? Now, choose some more patchwork pieces, here's a nice pink stripe and there's a blue and brown paisley print for you, and go and sit down at your desk.'

A week or two later, Dora felt sick at breakfast-time. Mother exclaimed at her paleness and sent her straight back to bed with Edwin's chamber-pot.

Dora had become almost resigned to these attacks. She knew it would go away in an hour or so, and lay seething inwardly at her ignorance. *How* could she find out what was wrong with her? Would she be ill every few weeks for the rest of her life? There must be a book somewhere which would tell her something.

Suddenly she remembered Edwin's croup, and Mother and Fanny and Lizzie with their heads in *Bull's Maternal Management* and *Consult Me*. *Bull's Maternal Management*, no, but *Consult Me For All You Want To Know, New Edition Improved by the Author of Enquire Within Upon Everything*?

She heard Fanny bringing Edwin upstairs to change into his outdoor trousers.

'Fanny!'

Fanny poked a cross head around the door. 'Yes, miss?'

'Miss *Dora*. Could you please bring me up *Consult Me*? It's on the kitchen mantlepiece.'

Fanny caught Edwin, picked him up and came in. 'I've got my hands full already, as you can see, without running up and down stairs for a malingerer. You shouldn't be wanting to read books if you're ill, you should be too weak to hold them.'

'Don't be so rude, Fanny! I'll tell Mrs Fishwick!'

'Oh, *will* you? And I'll tell Mrs Fishwick *too*, then! And what about my rise in wages?'

'I *will* speak to her about it, Fanny, honestly, but it didn't seem fair when she's so worried about Richard.' Dora hated to hear the whine in her voice.

'Well, just make sure you do, that's all. I'll tell Lizzie to bring that book up with your drink of milk at eleven o'clock.'

Dora lay back again, and reflected that Fanny would not be in a hurry to divulge her secret, because the moment she did so her hold on Dora would be lost.

Consult Me was irritatingly arranged in alphabetical order, *carpets* next to *caraway brandy* and *dying* next to *dysentery*. So if you did not know the name of what you were looking for, you had to begin at *abdominal ruptures* and carry on faithfully to *Yorkshire pudding* unless you were lucky enough to reach your destination somewhere in between. After several hours she had got as far as *funeral biscuits*. Then she heard the front door opening and voices in the hall.

There were footsteps on the landing, and a knock on the bedroom door. Miss Gossage appeared, carrying a tray.

'I have brought your afternoon tea, Dora. I hope you are well enough to take it? And I have brought you something else as well.' She handed Dora a letter.

'Thank you. Oh, it's from. . . . Did you tell Mother about it?'

'Of course not, Dora. I merely asked if I could see how you were. She is looking rather pale, I think. And how are you?'

Dora held the letter in both hands. 'I think I shall be recovered by tomorrow, Miss Gossage. It is very kind of you to come. You could have sent Betsy round on her way home.'

'I think not. Well, I will leave you with your letter and your tea. Goodbye, Dora.'

When she had gone, Dora waited a moment to see if her mother would come up. But there was silence. She took the letter, and opened it with the clean butter-knife.

'Dear Miss Fishwick,' she read. 'Once more I am

separated from home and family. It grieves me to be unable to comfort my poor mother. I think your friend was wrong about the progress of the war. I have heard it rumoured that there may come a big push that will end it all. The bluebells in the woods around the school are delightful.' Bluebells – daffodils – what a dolt he was! What about Humphrey? She could not entirely cease to care about Humphrey. . . . Ah! 'My father has received a postcard from Humphrey. It tells us little: it is printed with various messages, and he has underlined "I am quite well" and "I have received your letter". God be thanked that he has not been wounded. It was delightful to meet you once again. The summer term is very long. I may have a brief half-term break at Whitsuntide. I am, yours very sincerely, Alfred Bosanquet.'

She lay back. Phoebe was right. Humphrey was windy. He was so windy that he could not even write to his devoted father and his ailing mother. He was leaning against the side of the trench, hour after hour, day after day, mud-soaked and lice-ridden in the gas-filled air, sweating with terror while the brave tough Tommies went on watch and made tea and knocked off Huns all around him.

Thirteen

ONE DAY TOWARDS the end of May, Phoebe pounced out from the usual gateway and said, 'Bet you've forgotten!'

'I haven't, so there!' Dora held out a small brown parcel.

Phoebe tore it open. 'What is it? I know it's a book. I was sure you wouldn't remember. *Under the Greenwood Tree*! Oh, you devil! How super! How *did* you manage to get it?'

'Miss Gossage got it for me in town. She said, "Of course, Dora. There is scarcely anything I wouldn't do for the daughter of Mr Lofthouse." '

'Have you read it? What's it like?'

'Oh, it's lovely, but it's not so rum as *Far From the Madding Crowd.*'

'Are you really reading books that are *rum?* Dora, aren't we growing up? Dora, you'll never guess. Mother says that now I'm sixteen I can soon stop having lessons and start helping her at the hospital. Just imagine! Tending those poor soldiers, bandaging, emptying slop-buckets, scrubbing floors. . . .'

'But that's servants' work!'

'Mother says it's not going to be like that after the war. After all this is over, no one will be content to scrub anyone else's floors. Anyway, wouldn't you be thrilled to scrub floors for your precious Humphrey?'

'He's not my precious. . . .'

'Go on, you're blushing. But I won't mind any sort of dirty work at the hospital. It'll be something really *useful*, after all that poetry and mapping and chain-stitch. I mean, what are *you* going to do after you've finished at Miss Gossage's?'

Dora wished Phoebe wouldn't ask questions like that. This particular question had been skulking in the corners of her mind as if it were afraid of itself, and Dora had so far managed not to bring it out into the open. It wasn't fair, she thought, to bother Father and Mother with it at the moment. In any case, they would never let her do anything exciting. She would just stay at Miss Gossage's until she was seventeen, or even eighteen, like Hettie Bellerby. . . . What was Hettie Bellerby doing, though? Last year she was doing something called Prelim, and this year she was working for . . . what was it called?

'Well?' persisted Phoebe. 'Will you stay at home and embroider and learn how to give orders to Lizzie and Fanny? Unless Fanny's giving orders to you by that time.'

Dora said, with an air of confidence, 'I'm going to talk to Miss Gossage about the possibility of my taking some examinations.'

'Dora! Are you really? But what if you pass? And want to go to college or something? What would your father say?'

'I don't know. Phoebe, he's getting very morose. He spends most of his time sitting by the fireside, brooding. I couldn't talk to him about anything now. He doesn't even get angry with me. It's dreadful.'

'Anything from Richard?'

'Not a squeak.'

'Oh, *Dora.*'

They walked on in silence until they reached the corner.

'Dora. . . .'

'What? Come on, Phoebe, spill the beans. You've got that newsy look on your face.'

'No, don't be like that, Dora. It's awful.'

'Awful?'

'Well . . . I don't know if I ought to tell you. I mean, it might not be true, and in any case Richard might not be one of them.'

'One of *whom*? Oh, for pity's sake, Phoebe!'

Phoebe took Dora's hands. 'All right. But don't panic, will you?'

'I won't panic.' Oddly enough, she was sure that she wouldn't.

'Well, in last week's *Tribunal* it says that there's definite news of conscientious objectors being taken over to France. They're in the non-combatant corps, the one Richard had to join.'

'France – the military zone. That means, well, Miss Gossage says it means, that's where they get the worst punishments if they disobey orders.'

'Father says the death penalty.'

Dora said nothing. She had known that was what Miss Gossage meant. She felt a sudden sick sensation at the back of her throat.

Phoebe said miserably, 'What's happened to your beautiful bicycle, anyway? I thought you'd be riding it to school and back.'

'It needs oiling,' answered Dora. 'But Richard isn't here to oil it, and I can't ask Father. So there it sits, in the garden shed. I might never have had it as a birthday present at all.'

The next day, a Saturday, Mother had planned to take Dora to the Shop to buy her a new Sunday frock. But the day dawned wet and windy, and Mother was having one of her bad days.

'Then Dora's Sunday frock will have to wait,' said Father irritably at breakfast.

But as they set off for Hunstanby Road on Sunday, he took one look at Dora and said, 'I am ashamed to be seen with you, Dora. Look at the hem of your frock! It is almost. . . . Winifred! When is Dora to have a new Sunday frock?'

'As soon as we can manage to get to the Shop, my dear,' said Mother meekly.

'Then you will go to the Shop next week. I will alert Miss Mallinson to your needs. School? What does a day away from school matter? You will buy a new frock immediately, and that is the end of it.' And he limped out through the front door.

Dora had been feeling increasingly tender towards Father lately, but at this some of her customary anger returned. What did a day away from school matter, indeed? What did Dora's schooling matter at all, to Father? How could he even begin to contemplate allowing her to continue her education for years more at Miss Gossage's, and beyond?

She dreaded the visit to the Shop. She had not been there since Richard's arrest, and she wondered how the stalwart respect of the staff for the name of Fishwick had stood up to this scandalous blow. She would really rather go along the street to Rubbish and Grumble, but did not dare suggest this to Mother.

But Trapnell at the door, after a quick formal 'morning Mrs Fishwick, madam, morning Miss Dora' was almost bouncing up and down with excitement. 'Well, Jutland, Mrs Fishwick, madam! What do you think of it, then?'

Dora's mother was nonplussed. She too must have been expecting hostility on Richard's account. 'Oh! Jutland! I just don't know, Mr Trapnell. It all seems very confusing to me. And your sons? Any news of them?'

'Oh, Mrs Fishwick, our Billy's wounded, that's the youngest, but no, it's not sad, Mrs Fishwick, it's a Blighty one he's got, and he should be home within the week, they tell me.'

They passed on through the departments. Mother said a few words here and there, and Dora kept her eyes on the floor. At leather goods they stopped. 'Good morning, Mrs Barrow. Any news of Mr Grimes?'

Mrs Barrow was a pleasant dumpy widow with three daughters. Dora thought her a great improvement on Mr Grimes. 'Well, Mrs Fishwick, I don't rightly know. You see, his wife won't come in here or speak a word to us any more. Miss Hankinson was saying only yesterday that she saw young Harry in the street and he passed her by as if she was. . . . Well, no, I can't rightly say I've got news, no.' She looked uncomfortable and said, 'Miss Mallinson says Miss Dora is to have a new Sunday frock. Well, isn't that exciting, now.'

No one asks for news of Richard, she thought as they went upstairs. She wondered if any of them could imagine him as he was now, whether they had any notion of him being stripped naked and fed dry biscuits and water, or shipped willy nilly to Boulogne and given Field Punishment No. 1. Dora felt sick every time Phoebe's words about F.P. No. 1 came back into her mind: 'Tied to a steel cross-bar for hours at a time . . . unable to turn their heads without extreme pain . . . almost like crucifixion. . . .' But Phoebe was right, of course; he might not even be in France. He might be scrubbing the barrack-room floor at Felixstowe or even be still at Richmond Castle trying to persuade the soldiers of the evils of war. She did not know where he was; there was absolutely no way of finding out. Father and Mother too were in the dark, but they did not know about the men who had been sent to France. She felt the pressure of the responsibility of this knowledge, it weighed down upon her and oppressed her. As they walked towards thin, upright, efficient Miss Mallinson, with cream and white dresses over her arm, a picture came into her mind of Richard and Humphrey side by side before a firing-squad at Boulogne, one for conscientious disobedience and the other for desertion.

'This is nice, dear,' said Mother, 'with the broderie anglaise down the front. I think it's got the fullness that you need, here. . . .'

'Or this, Mrs Fishwick,' said Miss Mallinson crisply. 'This neckline would set off Miss Dora's complexion ideally. No, Derek, I can't speak to you now, can't you see I'm busy with Mrs Fishwick?'

But Derek the errand-boy still hovered nearby as the neckline was held up against Dora's complexion. He kept on muttering, 'Excuse me, excuse me, but Miss Mallinson.' He reminded Dora of her first term at Miss Gossage's when she had been too shy to ask if she could leave the classroom to go to the lavatory. Finally Dora's mother said, 'I think Derek is trying to give you a message that's rather urgent, Miss Mallinson. I assure you that we are in no particular hurry. Do attend to him, please.'

Miss Mallinson seemed put out, but said, 'Very well, Derek, what is it, but be quick about it, I haven't got all day.'

'Please, Miss Mallinson, a message has just come through, I think it was the newspaper boy brought it, he bumped into someone coming out of the post office, and it's news – yes, Mrs Fishwick madam, terrible news – what will we do without him, but Lord Kitchener's gone, madam! Yes, killed, they say! Drowned! Somewhere in Scotland! What a tragedy . . . trag . . . well, what a terrible thing for England, madam!'

'Drowned? Lord Kitchener? Mrs Fishwick, let me take those frocks from you. Mrs Cawley! Have you heard the news? It's Lord Kitchener! He's been drowned. . . .'

Dora thought, three quarters of an hour later when she was at last trying on the broderie anglaise, that England would never be the same again.

In the week before Whitsuntide, two things happened: Dr Fuller called on Father, and Mr Edwards from number 22 oiled Dora's bicycle.

Dr Fuller had not been called for, but had seen Father limping along the road and come of his own accord. After a moment's anger Father relented, and the two men, each grey with their own particular grief, went together into the drawing-room.

Later that evening, Dora sat in the drawing-room with her parents, quietly sewing in front of the empty grate and waiting for some mention to be made of the doctor's diagnosis. Mother sewed too, and Father was deep in volume six of the encyclopaedia, FOE to GOW.

Nothing was said.

'Pass me the scissors, would you, Dora?'

'Yes, Mother.'

Then she heard Fanny and Lizzie giggling on their way upstairs. 'Excuse me, Father, Mother.' She went out quickly and caught up with them on the landing.

'Fanny, Lizzie!'

Fanny stood back; she was not speaking to Dora at the moment. But Lizzie said, 'Yes, Miss Dora?'

'Please, Lizzie. I know you always manage, well, to go and offer a cup of something at just the right moment.'

'It's gout he's got, Miss Dora. Gout.'

Fanny, despite herself, giggled. 'Gout! I ask you! And him a total what d'you call it, and never touched a drop!'

'Yes, I'll be sent out for the ipecacuanha powder in the morning, just you see. Well, it's no wonder he's been looking bad, what with that and Mr Richard. Takes some beating, does that, doesn't it? Gout. Mr Fishwick with the gout. I ask you.'

Dora went back downstairs, filled with a great pity for Father. If he had been able to choose an illness that would shame and degrade him, he could not have found a better one. She heard him say as she entered the drawing-room, 'And so it is not always caused by . . .' but then he shut the encyclopaedia with a slam.

Mother said hastily, 'Arnold, dear, Dora was asking me, since her bicycle is now ready for her to ride again, she wondered whether she might ride out on it? During the Whitsuntide holiday, perhaps? You might ride round to the Fullers', mightn't you, dear, and encourage Betsy to take the air, for I believe she too has a bicycle.'

'Or even,' said Dora, glancing at her father's still impassive face, 'I might go out riding on my own. Just for a little ride – perhaps to the Green to practise going up hills and down again. I feel sure that if I ride regularly I'll soon become quite proficient. Minnie Chapman at school says that she goes out every day for a quarter of an hour except on Sundays and when it is raining, and her father says she is steady as a. . . .' She was going on and on, hoping for some response.

At last Father looked at her, turning his head slowly and not really seeming to see her. 'Ride your bicycle, Dora? No, I suppose I have no objection. Only mind your skirts on the chain. Winifred, I shall retire early. What a close evening. Do not sew too long, you will get one of your headaches. I wish you goodnight.'

Fourteen

THE CYCLE RIDE to the church was pure ecstasy. She was free, she was wicked, she was alone. She was a rabbit roaming on the hillside; she was a canary flying in an open sky.

She left her bicycle just inside the gate and walked up the gravel path, her heart pounding. It seemed so long since she had last been, since that fateful encounter with Alfred and Humphrey at Easter. The sun was brilliant in between the yew trees; the path was striped with shadows. The stained glass would be perfectly beautiful. Would Alfred be there? 'I may have a brief half-term break at Whitsuntide,' he had said. She listened for the sound of the organ music as she grasped the handle of the door.

No: all was quiet. There was probably nobody there. She closed the outer door, glanced down at her feet, decided to keep on her light summer shoes, and went into the church.

The sun, streaming through the yellow and red and blue of the east window, was spectacular. The light fell diagonally, mottling the choir-stalls on the left of the church and turning the blue velvet curtain that hid the organ into a patchwork quilt. For a moment she almost thought she heard the music of a Bach fugue coming from the pipes, so fused in her mind were these gorgeous colours with the intricate flow of sounds she had heard on her first visit to the church.

But there was no sound. And then there was a sound. There were footsteps inside the vestry, and coming out through the open vestry door. The familiar black-robed figure emerged from behind a pillar. He stared at her, but kept on walking towards her and turned round the corner of the pews till he was walking down the aisle.

He held out a hand. She took it, limply. 'Miss Fishwick.' His voice seemed deeper and more constrained than she remembered it. 'I have left the music and the boy here weekly. I trust you have not been unwell?'

'No, no.' What could she say? 'Circumstances, er, intervened to prevent me.'

Silence. Then, 'Have you news of your brother?'

'Richard?' She looked up at him. He was the first person, except Phoebe and Miss Gossage whom she supposed he would call Hun-coddlers, to have enquired after Richard. 'No, at least, only a letter shortly after his . . . after he went away. We do not know where he is. And your son?'

He turned, and started walking back towards the vestry. She was startled, but there was something in his manner which indicated that she should follow him. She did so, and as they approached the vestry door he half-turned and nodded to her. She wondered what could be awaiting her.

On the table where the Bibles and prayer-books lay was a pile of the flimsy greyish paper on which Humphrey wrote letters from the Front. The pile was about two inches high.

The rector sat down on one side of the table and gestured at the chair where she had sat before.

'But,' she said, sitting down, 'are these all from him?'

'Yes,' he said. She was right, his voice was deeper, heavier. It reminded her of Father's. 'These are letters which Humphrey has written since January. We have not received them until now. He did not send them. But a fellow officer, a friend of my son's, who happened to be passing through the town, called yesterday and gave them to me.'

'But why did he not send them? And why does he not

send them now? Why could he not post them? Is he all right – wounded – anything?' The questions came pouring out.

'He is . . . not wounded. He. . . .' For a moment the rector seemed unable to speak. Then he went on, 'These letters are about the war as he sees it. They . . . they would not pass the censor.'

'Censor?'

'All letters from the Front are read. These would be destroyed. They are shocking, horrifying. They do not accord with the picture of the war that we receive from customary sources. He wanted me to see them, so that I might understand.' He sounded dazed. 'He concludes by saying that he knows the war is shortly to take a new turn. There is to be an effort from which many men will not return.'

Dora stared at the pile of letters. A small glass paperweight held them down and stopped them, she thought, rising up towards her hand. She was hesitant: he did not ask her if she would like to read them. Would it be improper for her to ask if she may?

'I, er, I wondered, is Alfred at home for his mid-term holiday?'

'He is not. My wife is not well enough to have him at home at the moment. He has remained at school.'

She said cautiously, 'I am sorry that your wife is ill. I hope it is not serious?'

'Yes, it is,' he said. 'No, that is to say, it is not acute. But it is extremely debilitating.'

'I am so sorry.' She didn't dare look at him. She felt that her sympathy might be too much for him.

There was another silence, and she began to feel that she must soon leave. She stirred, but he said quickly, 'I would like you to read the letters.' He spoke as if asking her to do him a service. 'No, no, it would distress you too much.'

She said, 'You forget, sir, that my brother has made me well aware of the horrors of this war.' Her voice was quiet and astonishingly self-assured.

'Your *brother?*' He looked genuinely confused.

Dora felt her confidence waning and spoke quickly before it disappeared altogether. 'I think, perhaps, Richard and Humphrey would agree that war is not always heroic and glorious.'

She wondered if he were angry, and certainly he was still confused. 'Be that as it may,' he said. 'Perhaps you would read one or two of them.' He lifted the paperweight. 'Here is one from February – one from April – one from May.' Each letter comprised about a dozen sheets. He gave them to her. 'Would you please be good enough to return them at your earliest convenience? I am usually in the church at about this time. Well, goodbye, Miss Fishwick.'

As she went back down the aisle and out of the church, she made hurried plans to secrete the letters under her coat while she rode home on her bicycle and then to carry them somehow into the house and upstairs to her room.

Just inside the front door, Fanny was waiting to pounce.

'I can't wait much longer,' she hissed. 'Unless you go to your mam this very evening. . . . And what have you got there, anyway, trying to hide it behind your back?'

'A . . . a diary, kind of, it's . . . it's secret, I mean, private.' She blushed hideously.

'*More* secrets! I *shall* have a lot to tell her, won't I?'

'Oh, leave me alone, will you, Fanny! I will speak to her, really, truly. There, Edwin's screaming, you'd better go to him or Mother will say you're not doing your job properly.' She held the letters with her skirts and leapt up the stairs two at a time.

The letters were, in fact, more like a diary. There was no 'B.E.F. France' or 'Trenches'; just a date. The pages did not seem to be addressed to anyone. The writing was less tidy than in the letters she had read, and it sometimes deteriorated into a scribble.

The pages dated '20 February', she thought, must have

been written at about the same time as the letter about the Private from Heckmondwike. That letter had talked of parades and lectures. This one began: 'I know I must sleep all I can here, to build up my strength for the trenches. But sleep evades me. I seem to chase it down long dark corridors, trying to catch it, grabbing at it, but finding my grasp torn away by phantom rats and flying shrapnel. Sometimes I think I will cry out; once or twice I may have done so, for Dodsworth has asked me if I have had a bad dream. He is a stalwart, a real brick. He knows my standing with the men is low, and tells me they have no discrimination in these matters. I am sensitive, he says, I feel things deeply, which makes it my fate to suffer more than most. This comforts me somewhat; but when the men laugh and joke – I cannot write it down, it cuts me to the quick, the insults whispered behind the hand, the laughing obscenities. One man, a simple Private named Smith who has had two fingers shot off, came to me after one such episode today and said, "Not to fret yourself, sir, it's just their way of keeping their pecker up." I hope I showed my gratitude, for I truly felt it. I think I smiled, at least I made an attempt to smile, and I shook him by the hand as warmly as I could. It was his injured hand; I hope I did not let it go too hastily.'

There was more, much more. Dora glanced through the pages quickly. A lump was rising in her throat. 'Marching through villages . . . snow . . . man with foot swollen to three times its proper size, a bright pink lump . . . terrible tales of cruelty, lust and murder . . . appetite gone . . . rumours from the trenches. . . .'

She turned to the April letter, wondering if she would be strong enough to read it through, for it was from the trenches. It began: 'The only comfort in all this, strange to say, is the sky overhead. Stand-to being at dawn and dusk, we see, on days when it is not raining, the first light rising behind the German lines, that light which is pale and yet intense, sometimes a delicate turquoise, sometimes the sweet pale pink of those tiny translucent seashells we used to find on the shore at Whitby, sometimes a vivid almost flame-like orange. Then at dusk there lies behind us the violet haze of sunset, perhaps with steel-grey lines across it, perhaps clear, and fading upwards into the purest blue which deepens, is sparked by the first star, and leads up to the darkness of the night. Even when the clouds are thick and the unremitting rain torments us, I look up into that sky, and think of hymns sung in childhood about a Friend for little children, and ponder on those men in all the miles and miles of trenches up and down the Line who also look up into that relentless sky. Of those who look up into the sky from the strange territory on the other side of no-man's-land, I cannot bring myself to think, any more than I can think of those who sit by their fires at home in ignorance of how we suffer here.'

There was a pause at this point, and then some writing blotched with mud and then crossed out. It went on '. . . begin to think I am haunted. The clouds above me seem to be leering downwards towards the trench, pressing in like a great steel hand. I look down, and wonder if the moving mass I see in the trench, of mud and bodies and shell-holes filled with grey-brown water and unspeakable garbage, is also a haunting nightmare. I know it is not; but is the great steel hand which threatens me not also real? It comes to clasp me in its embrace even in sleep, though sleep is a word I have almost forgotten. When I lie attempting sleep, the rattle and bark of shell-fire, the flash of flare lights and the abominable pervasive smell of gas, all drag me back into grim wakefulness. When I am awake, the gripping fatigue paralyses my limbs and sends my mind into a seizure. So sleep is a grim wakefulness, and wakefulness a nightmarish sleep.'

She had seen him at Easter, she thought, possibly within days of his writing those words. Since then, there had been no word from him except the Field Service postcard. But he had kept on writing, writing words that were unacceptable to those presenting a different image of the war to the ones who had remained at home.

'16 May. Perhaps it is the 17, I do not know and am unconcerned. I am in mortal fear of losing my mind. Since returning from billet, I have thought that each night would be my last. I have pondered on the church's teaching on death, and on Heaven and Hell. I know that the all-consuming fire is my just desert. I care less and less for my fate and that of my men. I heard Private Smith say to me tonight as I stood, as in a trance, against the side of the trench: "Come on now, sir, this just won't do, will it? The men are waiting for their orders." I said something, I forget what. It is getting more and more difficult to write. I think I said, "Give them their orders then, you know what they should be doing, tell them I said so." He said, "Are you ill, sir?" but I could not reply because I did not know what he meant. I am ill, he is ill, we are all ill. There is nothing but sickness, vomiting, blood and death. There will never be anything else but death. Death, death – if it came I would smile to it – but when it comes I shall perish eternally. I shall die, die, die for ever and ever.'

There was more, but it was almost indecipherable, and in any case Dora folded the letters quickly at this point and put them down on the bed. The pain she felt for Humphrey was almost intolerable. She did not care that he was not gallant, could not lead men, lived in fear of his death. She no longer judged him. She felt the mud on his skin, the lice in his clothes, the wind and rain beating against his face. She felt that great steel hand closing in on her as it had done on him, squeezing out all hope and all vision and all warmth and comfort and well-being. She felt the closeness of death; his death could almost have been her own.

It was not until she heard her mother calling her for the third time that she realized that she must somehow account for her morning, face her mother's anxious frown, and then put over Fanny's case for a rise in wages.

Fifteen

SITTING MISERABLY in her bedroom five hours later, eating her tea – paste sandwiches, stewed prunes and warm milk, a real nursery tea – Dora reflected on the capriciousness of human nature. Time and again she had created in her imagination the scene when she would approach Mother about Fanny's wages, had pictured her responding with sadness at their inability to pay more, or with anger at Fanny for not realizing her extreme good fortune in serving the Fishwick household, or with puzzlement that the request should be made at all. What she had not expected was fury directed solely against herself.

Was fury the right word to describe Mother's outburst? Yes, she decided it was. Mother's was not the calm, bitter anger of Miss Gossage, or the leaden unquestioning disapprobation of Father. She had lashed out at Dora with accusation after accusation, lashing her with words as she had lashed Edwin with her hand in the frantic days between Nannie's departure and the engagement of Fanny.

'You have been gossiping with the servants about our financial position! You have lowered yourself, so that Fanny talks to you as if she were an intimate friend or relation! You have encouraged her to see your father and myself as niggardly and penny-pinching. You have given the girl ideas above her station, taught her airs. Worse, you have implied that her care of Edwin is such that it merits extra financial reward. As if I, his own mother, do not know his needs and whether they are or are not being met! As if Fanny cares for Edwin more than I do myself, as if she deserves more praise. . . .'

Dora was speechless in the face of this. She was aware that her hesitant remark about Fanny's wages being possibly due for revision had dropped a pebble into a pot simmering with other ingredients, but she could not sort out in her mind what those other ingredients were. She felt a little of that sick shame she had felt with Miss Gossage and the rector, but it was mixed with resentment that she should be blamed for the other ingredients in Mother's pot.

Now, of course, it remained to be seen what Mother would do next. She might tell Father; or, in his present mood, she might not. She might – for miracles do occasionally happen – think it over, decide she had been unjust, and give Fanny a few extra pounds after all. But it was most likely that she would summon Fanny, or even ask Father to summon Fanny, to tell her (politely, in case she gave notice) that she ought to consider her present wages quite satisfactory.

And what would Fanny say then? 'In that case, sir, madam, there are one or two things about the behaviour of Miss Dora that I think you ought to know.' No; Fanny was not unintelligent. She would be more subtle. She would go away, be sweet as honey for a day or two, and then quietly drop hints about Dora when they were discussing Edwin's bowel movements. Mother would prick up her ears: for all her strictures to Dora about gossiping with the servants, she could not resist a dropped hint. Then the cat, all the cats, would be out of the bag, and all the fury of the Fishwick parents, fuelled by the stress of the last few months, would be poured like boiling oil over Dora's head.

But what, she asked herself, is my suffering compared with the suffering of Humphrey Bosanquet? She wondered whether she was fit, in her present state of tension, to read his letters again. She decided that her own difficulties were in fact strengthening her to share his pain.

She got up and went over to the chest of drawers where she had hidden the letters between her camisoles and petticoats.

But as she passed the fireplace, she noticed on the mantlepiece the dark red volume she had been reading when Miss Gossage had come to visit her with Alfred's letter. She had only got as far as *funeral biscuits,* she remembered. The information she was seeking might be there, if only she had the patience to look.

She decided to sit and read *Consult Me* over her stewed prunes, and save Humphrey for when she drank her milk later on.

She had learned how to clean *very dirty kid gloves,* which was useful because the gloves Richard had given her for her birthday were in a disgraceful state, and she had learned, less usefully, how to make *horse ointment* with bee's wax and hog's lard and turpentine, and how to keep *ketchup* for twenty years without it spoiling. She began to flick crossly through the Ls and wonder whether the Ms and onwards were really worthwhile. She had finished her prunes and was itching to re-read Humphrey's letters. But then, after *melancholy* (see *hypochondria, p. 215*) and *melted butter,* she came across a word she did not recognize. *Menstruation,* she read. 'Menstruation is a natural secretion, of a red colour, from the womb, so named from its occurring once in a month.'

Once a month. . . . She read on. 'Menstruation begins from the fourteenth to the sixteenth year. But the circumstances of a female having passed the age of sixteen does not always demand medical aid. The date of puberty varies very widely, and one female may menstruate at twelve, and another at twenty years of age, without the health being impaired. The periodical discharge appears to be for the purpose of keeping up sanguification, or the making of blood in the body, for the purpose of gestation.'

Dora let the book sink on to her knee. Her hands were trembling. This was what she had been seeking; she was certain of it. This . . . this thing, this menstruation, was what her body was preparing for, this was what would happen to her when her body was ready for it. She snatched up the book again: 'Secretion, of a red colour' (blood?) '. . . puberty' (this seemed to be the name given to the time of onset – she, Dora, must be nearing puberty) '. . . sanguification . . . gestation' (what was that? She had never heard the word before).

It was wonderful, wonderful but maddening, maddening and frightening. She had known for so long that something was happening to her, had ignored it, fretted over it, had dreams at night over it – but here at last was a fact, to go along with the facts of her fainting attacks, her swelling figure and the mysterious hair appearing on different parts of her body. She, a female of sixteen, could expect a sanguification (which she understood because Miss Gossage had taught her girls the Latin derivations of English words) and a discharge. *When* she could expect it was clearly a matter of doubt. Unpredictability seemed to be the rule in this aspect of human nature too. And how infuriating not to know the real nature of the discharge, how long it would last, how to deal with it when it came. . . . She closed her eyes, and a vision rose before her of a thick red liquid flowing out of her body in the night, swamping the sheets, staining the carpet, congealing on the linoleum. She could not know when it would come. She could not control it, could she, like the urge to go to the lavatory when it was not appropriate? And it would happen once a month – but for how many years? For ever? When she was old, old as Mother and even as old as Grandmother Fishwick, whose grey face she remembered from early childhood – would she even then have to prepare herself each month for this unpredictable, undignified effusion from her body?

And for what purpose? 'For the purpose of gestation.' Quickly she thumbed back to the Gs; but no, between *gentian, tincture of*, and *gherkins, to pickle*, there was nothing.

Then there returned to her in a flash the words of Miss

Gossage on Latin derivations. 'Some English words,' she had said, 'are of uncertain derivation. Take the word gestation, for instance. Can any girl tell me what it means? Dora? No? It means the carrying of the child before it is born. Two Latin verbs come to mind here: *gestare*, to carry, and *gerere*, to bear. Each would be appropriate as the origin of gestation. I myself incline towards *gestare*, but it is open to you to disagree with me.'

So! This discharge, this monthly plague, was a preparation for the carrying of children. Dora let the book slip to the floor and put her head in her hands. She did not know whether to be in ecstasy or in terror. She could not think clearly; it was too much for her. She got up and went shakily over to the bed and lay, face downwards, for a long time.

She heard Father come in, she heard Fanny putting Edwin to bed, she heard footsteps on the stairs which were sometimes identifiable and sometimes not. Sometimes she listened, sometimes she just lay in a kind of daze, and for a few moments she actually dropped off to sleep. She lost track of the time, except that it was still light outside, but then it was almost exactly midsummer.

She was just beginning to get cold and to wonder whether she would be brought a hot drink before bedtime when there was a knock at the door.

She sat up quickly. 'Come in!'

It was Lizzie. 'Well, Miss Dora, your father and mother wishes to see you in the drawing-room. You do look pale, then – been just lying on your bed, have you? Not even drunk the milk I warmed for you. Well, I'll take these things down. I'll say you're just straightening your frock, shall I?'

The grandfather clock showed five minutes to eight as she went past it. She felt quite calm, and wondered if this was how soldiers felt when they went over the top. She knew she would be punished; the only questions were, for how many offences, and how long and how severe the punishment would be. She remembered that when she was about seven her father had hit her on the hand six times with a ruler for denying that she had stolen a teaspoonful of jam. She had been aware that he had detested hitting her and hated himself for doing it.

She went into the drawing-room and found Mother sitting down and looking tearful, Father standing looking troubled in front of the fire-screen, and Fanny facing them and appearing to hide a smile behind her hand.

'Come here, Dora.'

'Yes, Father.' She stood in front of him in such a position that she could not see Fanny.

'It appears, Dora . . .' he sounded tired '. . . it appears that you have discussed with your mother some matters which ought properly to concern only Fanny and myself. Those matters have now been dealt with to my satisfaction. But Fanny has raised another matter, which has shocked us deeply.' He looked over Dora's shoulder. 'Perhaps you could repeat to Miss Dora, Fanny, what you told us.'

Fanny came nearer to Dora, but Dora still did not look at her.

'Well, I had to tell them, didn't I, Miss Dora? I mean, it wasn't right, you going out and cycling with Miss Phoebe and walking with her back from school and *enticing* Mr Richard along there when you knew you'd been told not to. I've held my peace so long as I could, Miss Dora, but really, there's right and there's wrong and. . . .'

'And there is vindictiveness, Fanny.' Father's voice held some of the old sharpness.

'Beg pardon, sir?'

'Vindictiveness. You asked for a rise in wages, in fact you induced Miss Dora to make the request for you. The request failed, so you accuse Miss Dora.'

'I . . . well, I'm speechless! Sir, madam, I ask you, am I the sort of person who. . . ?'

'You should say no more, Fanny, if you wish to receive a satisfactory recommendation from me for your next position. Be that as it may. I still have to deal with you,

Dora.' He turned to her, and the tiredness seemed to sweep over him again. He stood straight, appearing to have been cured of his pain for the moment by Dr Fuller's medicine, but the lines on his face were deeply drawn and his eyes were dark and sunken. 'You have betrayed the trust we had in you, Dora. You knew that Mr Lofthouse was, in part, responsible for the position in which Richard now is. And considering that we had even gone to length of ceasing to attend his chapel. . . .'

'But he supported Richard, defended him at his trial! I mean, tribunal.'

Father raised his voice. 'You had been forbidden to visit the manse. You had been forbidden to associate with that family. Your own opinion on the matter is irrelevant. While you live under this roof you will do as I say.'

If only I could answer him, argue with him, face him as Richard did! thought Dora. But I am weak, cowardly, a female, subject to fainting attacks and sudden bodily secretions. She struggled to find the words to say, and knew that they would only come to her later, upstairs, when she had already meekly accepted her punishment.

'You will be confined to your room for the rest of the Whitsuntide holiday. Your meals will be brought up to you by Lizzie. Your mother and I will provide you with suitable literature to occupy your time. The next occasion on which we will see you downstairs will be when you come with us to chapel on Sunday. Goodnight, Dora.'

Fanny remained in the drawing-room after she left. Dora heard Father say, wearily, 'Now, Fanny . . . ' before she shut the door.

Sixteen

DORA TRIED TO write her diary; it was impossible. She got up, paced across the room, looked out of the window into the garden. She picked up *Tales to Lead the Young along the Way* and put it down again. She picked up Tennyson, was momentarily absorbed –

> On either side the river lie
> Long fields of barley and of rye
> That clothe the wold and meet the sky;
> And through the field the road runs by
> To many-tower'd Camelot

– but it was too gracious, too ordered, elegant, calm, flowing. Her own thoughts seemed to creep along sluggishly, fall to the depths, be wrenched back upwards, take a leap to the heights, fall and fall and creep along again, wearily.

She had endured two days of imprisonment: she could not imagine how she could survive another four. She looked out of the window again, saw the shed in which her bicycle languished, and turned away. The sun streamed in through the window. Her shadow fell in front of her, dark and sharp on the patterned blue carpet.

She made plans for escape. Opening the window, she looked down: from her window-sill the wall plummeted to the ground. No convenient lean-to roof, as she was sure Katy or the March sisters would have found; no Virginia creeper for an escape in the style of Stalky. If she jumped, she would break most of her bones, including probably her neck. Such a fate would not be tragedy, it would be humiliation.

There was no escape by stealth. But could she not summon them to her and say, 'The offence for which you have been punishing me has brought me news of Richard.' She could see their pale faces, eager for news, yet dreading it. 'He may be in France, awaiting execution by firing-squad.' But she could not do it. It was partly that her information was too flimsy, but (and here her own altruism surprised her) she could not bear to hurt them so deeply.

She went again, for the fifteenth or twentieth time, to the drawer to find Humphrey's letters. She would have to return them, at her 'earliest convenience'. She lifted the petticoats and just stared at them. It was hardly worth taking them out, because she knew them almost by heart. She put out a finger and touched them. It gave her the feeling of touching the mud and the horror of war. She tried to picture, quite realistically, a trench on the Western Front. The long lines of cheery or despairing men, the morning rum ration, the rats scurrying over food and sleeping bodies and laid-down rifles, the gas-masks that stifled breathing, coils of barbed wire, flying pieces of shrapnel, rain, duckboards, itching, sweat, filth, sleeplessness, the constant smell of death.

She suddenly thought of Humphrey's mother. Mrs Bosanquet, it seemed, was never well, never spoke to anyone, never went out. She was like Dora, imprisoned, but by no one but herself. 'Before the war,' Alfred had said, 'she just thought we might get knocked down by a motor car. Now she's sure that Humphrey's going to get done for by the Boche.'

She must have lived for years in the constant presence of death. It had prevented her from taking part in life at all. Dora could hardly imagine it. Death – yes, it was horrifying, nightmarish. But before it came, was not life something to be seized and lived and gloried in? The glory of life had never burst upon Mrs Bosanquet. She must almost long for death as one might long to shake hands with a friend with whom one has corresponded but never met.

She let the petticoats go, shut the drawer, and sat down again in her chair. After a few minutes she reached out for *Consult Me* from the mantlepiece. Avoiding *menstruation,* which she was trying not to think about, she looked morbidly through the diseases: *cancer* ('to cure: use the cold bath, this has cured many'), *convulsions* ('give an aperient, such as magnesia and rhubarb'), *consumption* ('stimulating liniments and a medicated vapour bath'). No disease seemed to be incurable or to end in death, though with consumption 'emaciation rapidly increases, and the patient has alternations of hope and fear as to recovery. Hope, however, the most prevails'.

Eventually she found an entry called *whist* and read it avidly. She did not entirely understand it, but it was clear that whist was a game played with cards, and of that she knew her parents would totally disapprove.

By Friday she was beginning to wonder whether she was becoming insane, like Mrs Rochester in *Jane Eyre*. Her only visitor had been Lizzie with trays of unappetizing food, and Lizzie, not wanting to offend either Fanny or Mr and Mrs Fishwick, said little and kept her expression as solid as a rock. Dora knew that her mother would be pining for her company, but was submissive to Father's orders.

Release came, and from an unexpected source. On Friday morning, quite early, the doorbell rang. There had been few callers during the week, so far as Dora had heard; only the usual deliveries and the post-boy with letters of no significance. The post-boy had already been that morning, and social callers would not come till later. Dora put her ear to the bedroom door.

The front door was opened. There were voices, female voices, but the words were indistinguishable. In a moment, however, the front door was closed again, and Mother's unmistakably anxious tones emerged from the drawing-room. The incoming voice was raised in greeting. Dora knew it: it was Mrs Lofthouse.

She heard the drawing-room door close, and Lizzie's feet padding back to the kitchen. She sat down on the bedside chair, rigid with expectation. Had Mrs Lofthouse come with news of Richard, through Mr Lofthouse's pacifist organization? Was Richard in England, in France, in prison, alive? Had she come to beg for Dora's release, and for renewed friendship between the two families? Or had she merely come to say that Hammerton Square Chapel had been unable to find a treasurer to replace Father, and please would Mother try to persuade him to return?

After what seemed like hours, she heard the drawing-room door open again and their footsteps and voices on the stairs. Mother was talking quietly, and even Mrs Lofthouse sounded subdued.

There was a knock on the bedroom door. Dora leaped up and went to the end of the bed. 'Come in!'

Mother entered, followed by Mrs Lofthouse.

'Dora dear. . . .'

Dora came forward, and her mother held her and kissed her.

'Dora, Mrs Lofthouse has come.'

She shook hands with Mrs Lofthouse, shyly.

'How are you, my dear?' said Mrs Lofthouse, and at the warmth of her voice Dora felt instantly confident. 'What a pity there should have been such trouble between us, Lofthouses and Fishwicks. I'm sure it's not really necessary at all, only a few misunderstandings that have to be cleared up. Mr Lofthouse is going to speak with your father, but I thought I would come along and have a talk with your mother and yourself, just to till the soil, so to speak, before the seed is sown!'

'Is is true, Dora,' asked her mother urgently, 'that Phoebe told you some men in Richard's position had been sent over to France and might be in danger, well, in danger of their lives?'

'Yes, Mother, she did. I did want to tell you, I was so

afraid for Richard, but it might not have been him anyway and I couldn't bear you to worry and in any case. . . . But what has happened? Is there any news?'

Mother turned to Mrs Lofthouse, who said gently, 'Well, yes, Dora. It isn't news specifically about Richard, but it seems to tell us that at any rate the worst has not happened.' She sat on the bed, comfortably, and patted the bed beside her. Dora sat down, and Mother sat on the bedside chair. 'It seems that several contingents of the Non-Combatant Corps have been sent over to France with conscientious objectors among them. At least one of these contingents was from Richmond Castle, where Richard was originally sent.' Mrs Lofthouse was speaking unusually slowly and clearly; it reminded Dora of being taught to recite poetry. 'Once in France, of course, any man who disobeys orders is liable to the death penalty. And conscientious objectors have no alternative but to disobey military orders. It appears that some of them were indeed sentenced to death. We do not yet know any of their names, or even how many of them are in that position. But we have received definite information that the death sentences have been commuted – that is, that the men have not been shot and will not be shot, but are to be imprisoned for life instead.'

'Mrs Lofthouse couldn't bear,' Mother broke in, 'for you to be waiting, worrying, wondering whether Richard was safe or not. She did not know whether you had told us what Phoebe had told you. She says Phoebe has been cycling up and down past the end of Heathgate for days hoping to see you ride out. Oh, Dora, if only you had explained!'

'Come, Winifred my dear,' said Mrs Lofthouse, '– I may call you Winifred, mayn't I, as in the old days? – let us forget the quarrel between us, and Dora's punishment, and the offence that provoked it. What matters now is that we are united in our concern for Richard's safety and welfare, and Raymond will come this evening and try to win Arnold over, a task not without its difficulties no doubt, but Raymond has faced tasks that are infinitely more difficult in his time, so we will look to the future and hope to see smiles flowing between the two families once more, don't you think? Now, Dora will be longing to see what the downstairs of the Fishwick abode looks like again, won't you, Dora dear, after such a long absence? I think you said Lizzie might be making us a cup of coffee, Winifred, and she might bring an extra cup for Dora, mightn't she, perhaps?'

Chapel on Sunday was quite an event. Dora found a moment in which to wonder what Mr Cranston thought of their vacant seats at Hunstanby Road, but for the most part she was debating whether to stare straight at the members of the congregation or to look shyly down at the floor. She opted for the first, simply because she was so happy to be out of her prison and in communication with the Lofthouses again.

They were taken aback to find their pew occupied by a new family, but since there was half a pew vacant directly behind Mrs Lofthouse and Phoebe and her sisters, they went to sit there. Dora sang all the hymns lustily: at one point Phoebe half-turned and nearly giggled at her.

Father had seemed far from happy on their way to Hammerton Square, but Dora knew that he would fix any approaching interrogators with such a challenging stare as to make them merely stammer out, 'Glad to see you, Mr Fishwick.' He was still troubled sporadically by gout. Mother told Dora that Dr Fuller had said it would probably be with him for the rest of his life. There was a time when Dr Fuller had been famed for saying, 'It'll be gone in a trice, never fear!' Now it seemed that he believed in honesty rather than optimism.

Dora and Phoebe had spent all Saturday talking and cycling and talking again. Dora had shown Phoebe the entry in *Consult Me* and Phoebe had said, 'You mean to say you didn't know about *that*?' Whereupon Dora stifled her jealousy of Phoebe's superior knowledge and learned all the details of the condition and how to live tolerably while it lasted. Phoebe had found the Oxford Book open at Tennyson and collapsed with laughter, saying, 'It's all about it, didn't you know? "Out flew the web and floated wide; The mirror cracked from side to side; 'the curse is come upon me!' cried The Lady of Shalott." ' It took Dora a few minutes to tumble to what Phoebe meant, but having done so she decided that a 'curse' was indeed what this monthly visitor would turn out to be. On the other hand, she was relieved to learn that by Mother's age the thing would decide of its own accord that enough was enough. Phoebe said that this time tended to be rather trying for many women. Dora found it enlightening to find another reason, beyond Edwin's vitality, Fanny's unsuitability and Father's intractability, for Mother's bad days.

Father had been extraordinarily and obviously grateful to Mr Lofthouse for the information about Richard. Of course, they were no better informed about where Richard actually was now, whether he was among those men in France, or whether he was still in England and if so under what conditions he was being held. But on Saturday at breakfast Father had read out from the *Yorkshire Post* an item concerning conscientious objectors. By a government directive, conscientious objectors were no longer to be sent to military prisons, but to civil ones instead.

'Like Armley?' Mother was horrified.

'It is the easier option,' replied Father. 'They will receive only the same punishment as for a civil offence. No doubt some will say the government is being soft with shirkers. But,' he said, pushing his chair out from the table and crossing one leg carefully over the other, 'whatever may be said of other pacifists, I do not consider Richard to be a shirker. Cowards there may be, but Richard is not one of them.'

Well, Richard, thought Dora, wherever you may be, here is one battle that you have fought and won. She hoped that one day he would be in a position to learn about it.

Seventeen

'SO,' ASKED MISS GOSSAGE, 'what has Mr Lofthouse said he can do about it?'

They were sitting quietly in the schoolroom after everyone else had gone home. The room looked out on to Miss Gossage's wild back garden, where some starlings were fighting noisily.

'Well, he says he has friends with influence, Miss Gossage. Do you think he means Members of Parliament?'

'He may do. There are several who will take up the cases of conscientious objectors: Philip Snowden, for instance, and Edmund Harvey, and one or two others. But, of course, you are not seeking Richard's release, are you, you are merely seeking information. That is easier.' Dora felt privileged to be included in that 'you', the group of dedicated people determined to discover the truth about Richard. 'It is puzzling that you have received no letters from him. Conscientious objectors have usually been able to communicate with their families by some means or other, unless they are subject to unusual restraints.'

They sat silent for a moment. 'Unusual restraints' was an ominous phrase, and Dora pondered over it.

'Well,' said Miss Gossage at last, 'at any rate Mr Tennant has had to eat a small portion of humble pie in the House.'

'Mr Tennant?'

'The Under Secretary of State for War. He said last week that of course there was no question of pacifists being sentenced to death. Then a few days later he had to admit that there *had* been death sentences, though they had subsequently been commuted. You are smiling, Dora. Are you amused that I can be pleased at a man's humiliation? I am afraid that I *am* pleased, yes, gratified by it, and not in the least ashamed of my gratitude. I would like to feel guilty that I am not ashamed, but I do not. What a tortuous business it all is, isn't it. So you had a rather difficult half-term holiday?'

'Rather.' Dora had explained, by no means in every detail, that her parents had objected to her friendship with Phoebe, hence her confinement to her room.

'But why did they not object at the time of your brother's tribunal, when your father first realized the full consequences of Mr Lofthouse's influence?'

'Oh, he did. But he did not realize that I was still seeing Phoebe.'

'I see. And he found out last week? How?'

'It was Fanny, who looks after Edwin. She knew about it, and said she would tell Mother and Father if. . . .' There was another silence, an uncomfortable one.

'If what, Dora?'

'Well, if I did not do something for her.'

'Such as?'

Dora said quickly, 'Ask for a rise in her wages.'

'That, Dora, is called blackmail. It is a crime.'

'That's what Phoebe said, Miss Gossage.'

'Phoebe is a sensible girl. Dora, in some ways you are afraid of your parents, are you not?'

Dora hesitated, but then admitted that she was.

'Well, we are all afraid of somebody. I am rather afraid of Mr Babcock at King Edward VII's School for Boys. But fear can sometimes make people act against their common sense.' Miss Gossage began to tidy up her desk, or rather to move books and papers from one part of the desk to another, which did not make it any tidier. 'However, it all worked out well in your case, Dora. Unless, of course, there is anything *more* that Fanny knows and which you do not wish your parents to know. Dora, I have to tell you that your face is like an open book. How infuriating for you, though actually it is a very endearing characteristic. You are blushing. Fanny does know more. Do you want to tell me? I confess to being curious, but I must try to respect my own principles on privacy.'

'Oh, how can I tell you, Miss Gossage? It's all so confusing. I should never have got involved with them, it's none of my business, but people are . . . people are suffering, may be going to be killed, and other people are going to be so upset, it'll be more than they'll be able to bear. . . .' And Dora burst into tears. She wept and wept, on and on, absorbed in the physical business of weeping, the huge amount of wetness, the running nose, the hot stinging eyes, the feeling that the whole of her face was burning with flame. Miss Gossage sat quietly, saying nothing but handing her a handkerchief when her own was sodden and then another when that too was used up. Dora would have liked Miss Gossage to put an arm around her, but she did not.

When she finally emerged from her tears she found Miss Gossage looking at her with the utmost sympathy.

'It is the Bosanquet family, is it not? Yes, I thought so. I have been intrigued by them myself. Mrs Bosanquet practically a recluse, the rector so cold and impersonal. . . .'

'But he is not!'

'Oh?' Miss Gossage's eyebrows shot up. 'Is he not?'

'Oh, no! He worries terribly about his wife, and he cares deeply for Humphrey. I'm not sure how much he likes Alfred. . . .'

'He seems to have confided in you a great deal.'

Dora was embarrassed. Her face was still red from crying, and she remembered her open book face, which made things worse. 'Well, I went there to play the organ, you see, and I was interested in Humphrey, and I wasn't a member of his congregation so I suppose he knew I wouldn't tell any of them. And he has no one else to turn to, has he, with his wife being like that? I think Humphrey is really the one person he cares most about in the whole world, it's like Mother and Father with Richard, he's terrified that he'll be killed, because there may be a big push coming up. . . .'

Miss Gossage asked, catching her off balance, 'Do your parents care for Richard and not for you?'

'No, I don't mean that at all, I know they care for me and Edwin, I didn't mean that at all.'

'Good, good. But it has been a great burden to you to share this fear of Mr Bosanquet's?'

Dora realized for the first time that it had. Oh, it had been a privilege and an excitement too, but it was indeed a burden. She began to feel suddenly sorry for herself, a mere girl caught up in the whirlpool of international tragedy, and tears threatened again.

Miss Gossage said, practically, 'And Fanny knows something of this?'

'She knows about the first time I met Alfred, and that I have seen Alfred and Humphrey since. Well, no, she only saw Alfred.'

'And your parents would strongly disapprove of the association? Yes, I can imagine that they could, on many grounds.'

'Yes.'

Miss Gossage stood up. 'Well, Dora, I can give you one piece of advice, and it will be very hard for you to carry out. Fanny will no doubt tell your parents sooner or later, so you must tell them first. I know how you must feel about that. But I think your parents respect honesty and courage as much as I do, so in the end it will be for the best. Now, here is something that will take your mind away from it to some extent. Take these three volumes. I'm sorry they are so heavy. They are *War and Peace* by Leo Tolstoy. They should keep you busy for a little while, if you are confined to your bedroom again.' Dora took the books. 'Good, you can smile. I am glad to see it. Now you must be getting home.'

'What is that you are reading, dear? It looks very serious. I wonder if your father will be late back from his meeting? I feel rather tired, perhaps I will go to bed early. But it is so good to know he is back at chapel again.'

Dora stirred in her chair. She used to curl up with her book on the hearth-rug, but now she preferred a chair. 'It's something Miss Gossage lent me,' she said. 'About Napoleon, and Russia.' She was actually reading volume two. Miss Gossage had warned her that the characters were numerous and confusing, and since she was so good at selecting she might be best to concentrate on the parts about Natasha and Andrei and Pierre. Yesterday evening she had been enchanted by Natasha at the ball; now she had leapt through Natasha's downfall and was deep in the battle of Borodino.

She had skipped through a great deal of the book, she admitted, but at this point the story seized her imagination. She read every single word of it. She could picture it all, the meadows of new-mown hay, the cavalry and the infantry, batteries and redoubts – and then, with a shock, she came across the word *trench.*

Trench! *That* was why she was gripped; she was imagining the battle in which Humphrey and his men and so many others might shortly take part. 'A shell tore up the earth two paces from Pierre.' Two paces from Humphrey – and the next one might be no paces at all. 'Suddenly a frightful concussion flung him backwards to the ground. At the same moment he was dazzled by a great flash of fire, and a deafening roar and a hiss and a crash set his ears ringing.' But he was not dead. 'Beside himself with terror, Pierre leaped up and ran back to the battery which was the one refuge from the horrors surrounding him . . . he dashed downhill, stumbling over the dead and wounded who seemed to be catching at his feet. . . . Crowds of wounded walked or crawled or were carried on stretchers, their faces twisted in agony. . . .'

'Dora, dear! What on earth is the matter? There are tears pouring down your cheeks!'

Dora wrenched herself away from Pierre's and Humphrey's tragedy. She sniffed, and was angry with herself. 'I'm sorry, Mother. It's very, very sad. Have you a clean hankie I could borrow?' To cry twice, in a matter of days, first in front of Miss Gossage and then in front of Mother! She was not ordinarily a crying person. She was one who went upstairs and beat her pillow in a fury. She must try to pull herself together.

'No, dear, I haven't. I'm really rather short of hankies, I must ask your great-aunt Marion to send me some for my birthday. Go and fetch one out of your own drawer, dear.'

Dora got up, put down her book and went upstairs. She took a stout linen handkerchief from her top drawer and looked at herself in the mirror.

'I will regain my composure,' she thought, 'and then I will go downstairs and I will tell Mother about my association with the Bosanquet family. If Father comes in, I will tell him also.' Fanny had kept almost completely out of Dora's way since the other exposure, and this seemed almost as threatening as constant nagging and significant looks. 'I wonder,' she thought, looking at her eyes and thinking that their puffiness was receding, 'whether Father will be early or late. It certainly would be more convenient if he came in after my bedtime, so that Mother could break it to him gently. Then he would have time to sleep on it, too, before administering punishment.'

Then all of a sudden she began to feel extremely queasy. Her image swam before her in the mirror and she held on tight to the chest of drawers. She knew that she must get to the lavatory; her knees felt weak and trembling, but she almost ran out of the bedroom door, along the landing and around the corner. Rapidly, trembling all over now, she hitched up her skirts and pulled down her bloomers and sat down.

She must have sat there several minutes, the sickness fading and her breathing steadying and her brain clearing, before she noticed a mark on the inside of her bloomers.

She gasped, and looked down into the lavatory bowl. There it was, in the water: 'a natural secretion of a red colour.' It was hers. This was the secretion for the purpose of gestation. It had come now, and she had to deal with it.

She sat there for a few more moments, filled with a mixture of elation and fear. She had the sensation of being adult, of being in charge, of being a potential mother.

But then she thought, 'This is blood. I am bleeding.' She saw the men on the battlefields, of the men lying in pools of their own blood at Ypres, at Verdun, at that unknown place where men were going to fight, perhaps were fighting even now on the Western Front. What did it feel like, to be bleeding to death? 'I cannot die, I do not want to die,' Tolstoy's Andrei had thought. 'I love life – I love this grass, this earth, this air. . . .'

She wondered when she stood up if she would feel dizzy again, but she did not. She was dazed but quite calm. She took the handkerchief and placed it appropriately until she could find something more suitable. Then she went back to her room to find a clean pair of bloomers. Beside the bloomers in her drawer lay her petticoats, under which were hidden Humphrey's letters. She was tempted to touch the petticoats and murmur 'Humphrey!' but told herself briskly that it would be sheer sentimentality. In any case, she was in too much of a hurry to go and ask her mother where she could find large quantities of cotton wool.

Eighteen

DORA HAD TO get up very early the next morning, long before anyone else was awake, because of her own private preoccupations. She completed her task and came out of the lavatory quietly.

She and Fanny almost collided. 'Fanny!'

'Miss Dora!'

Their gasps both came out in shocked whispers.

Dora was so surprised that she forgot to be embarrassed. 'It's only a quarter past six! What's that you're . . . Fanny! That bag's full of your things!' She suddenly saw the misery and fear on Fanny's face. 'You're not *going*?'

'Course I am, Miss Dora. Didn't you know? Your pa gave me notice over that other business.'

Dora stared. 'Why didn't you tell me? Why didn't *they* tell me? Where are you going? Who will look after Edwin?'

'Your mam says she will herself. I'm going back to my nan's.'

'Your nan's?'

'She lives down by the railway. She won't want me, but she'll have no choice, will she? I'll tell her I'm just stopping. Anyway, I'll get another position. They gave me this.' She handed Dora an envelope.

The envelope contained a letter in Father's square handwriting which read: 'Miss Fanny Moon has been a Mother's Help in this house for six months. She can carry out simple tasks under supervision. She has an affectionate disposition.' Dora detected Mother's influence here. 'She should not be engaged in any employment that requires either self-discipline or the discipline of infants. Signed, Arnold Fishwick.'

'Oh, Fanny!' She realized that Fanny could not read the letter, and that she had no notion of the impression it would give to a future employer. 'Fanny. . . .' Dora couldn't restrain her curiosity. 'Fanny, you haven't *stolen* anything, have you?'

Fanny nearly dropped her bag. 'How did you know?'

'You have?' Their whispers were starting to get hoarse. 'Well, it's just that, in a recommendation, they usually actually *say* that someone is honest, and if they don't. . . .'

'They haven't gone and said I'm *not* honest?'

'No, no, they wouldn't do that. They've said you can do some jobs well, and . . . Fanny, Edwin's going to miss you.'

'I'll miss him, Miss Dora.' There were tears in her eyes. 'Go on, let me go, Miss Dora, I'm going now because I can't bear to kiss him goodbye.'

Dora had been standing in Fanny's way. She moved, and Fanny went past, knocking her with the string shopping-bag that contained all her possessions.

'Goodbye.' She watched Fanny for a moment, but then half-ran down after her and grabbed her arm at the bottom of the stairs.

'Fanny, just a minute!'

'Ssh!'

'Did you,' Dora whispered, 'did you tell my parents anything . . . anything more?'

'Let me go, Miss Dora. They'll hear you, let me go.' Fanny tugged away. 'I'm not telling you what they know. You're not worth it, you've never done anything for me. You'll get into trouble, I'll tell you that, with all your antics. I'm well rid of the Fishwicks, I'll tell everyone that, I'm well rid of you all. Oh Gawd, now look at this door, you'll have to help me with it, Miss Dora. Only don't bang it behind me, will you? I'm not a bad girl, Miss Dora, really. Look after Master Edwin for me, won't you?'

She was crying. Dora shut the door softly behind her. She wondered whether she should have searched the bag to see if the silver napkin-rings were in it, but thought that Fanny deserved some reward for loving Edwin, if for nothing else.

If Dora had been in Mother's position, she would have told Edwin that Fanny was unwell, or had gone away for a few days' holiday. But what Miss Gossage said was true: her parents placed a high value on honesty.

Struggling to push Edwin into his sailor-suit, Mother said, 'We have sent Fanny away, dear. She wasn't a very good person, and we thought we could manage quite well without her.'

Edwin was puzzled. He stopped resisting the sailor-suit while he concentrated on the problem. 'Who's a good person? I don't want a good person. Fanny shouldn't go away. I want Fanny.'

'Come on, Edwin, put that leg in here,' said Dora, who was helping because it was Saturday and there was no Miss Gossage's.

'We'll manage very well without Fanny, dear, don't you worry. Dora, did you see her go?'

'See her go! See her go! I want to see her go!' One leg still half-in and half-out of his trousers, Edwin escaped and ran around the nursery screaming, 'I want Fanny! Goodbye Fanny! Fanny didn't say goodbye! Want to see her go!'

It was a trying day. Dora helped Mother as best she could, but lost patience very easily. Lizzie said nothing at all about Fanny's departure and did not offer to help with Edwin in the morning, but after lunch she said, 'I wonder if the park'd be nice for him, Mrs Fishwick? It's rightly my afternoon off, and I could just do with a stroll myself. I've some crusts as'd be fine for the ducks.'

Mother was deeply grateful, and asked Dora if she would cycle to the corner shop for two ounces of peppermint creams, Lizzie's favourites, while she herself went and had a lie down. Dora felt very tired and heavy, and went for a lie down herself after her walk (cycling was out of the question) to the shop.

Lying on the bed, shifting to try to find the most comfortable position, she forced herself to think about Fanny, her father, the Bosanquet family, and what Miss Gossage had advised her to do. What, oh what had Fanny told her parents? Father had said little at breakfast that morning, but then he never did. Interviews, reprimands and punishments always took place in the evening when Father could give his full mind to them. Mother had not said anything, but she was fully occupied with Edwin.

She could imagine what would happen. They would have dinner, formally and silently. Lizzie would bring coffee into the drawing-room. Father would drink his coffee, place his cup and saucer carefully on the small table and say, 'Dora, there is a matter I must discuss with you.'

There was a look that sometimes came on to his face which frightened her. She had first been aware of it at the time of the jam episode, and several subsequent occasions had fixed it in her mind as 'that look'. It had been provoked many times in the early months of the year by Richard, and she had seen for the first time that the look was not only frightening but was actually caused by fear. When this thought had first crossed her mind, her reaction was: 'Father *frightened*? No!' But it was true. There were times when Father did seem full of fear. Somehow this made 'that look' seem even more frightening. Dora dreaded producing that look.

She got up when she heard Mother stirring, and helped Lizzie with nursery tea. Mother insisted on bathing Edwin herself, and though Lizzie and Dora, passing each other in the hall, exchanged glances at the noises issuing from the bathroom, neither of them interfered. Edwin was put to bed, Father returned from the Shop, and dinner took place in exactly the style that Dora's imagination had predicted.

Saturday was the day in between Friday's fish and Sunday's mutton. Dora waited until Lizzie had produced cheese pudding, mashed potatoes and peas, and then she spoke.

'Father,' she said, and then had to clear her throat. She began again. 'Father, I wonder if the *Yorkshire Post* has given you any recent information about the progress of the war? I happened to meet a most interesting young man recently whose brother is an officer in the Second York and Lancaster Regiment, and he had heard it rumoured that the war is shortly to take a new turn.'

'Dora, who in the world . . . ?' her mother began.

'Indeed!' Her father laid down his knife and fork and looked at her from under his eyebrows. 'The situation at the Western Front makes you anxious, does it, Dora? Of course, the whole nation was downcast at the losses at Verdun and the death of Lord Kitchener. But Haig knows what he is doing out there. Of that I am convinced.' He picked up his knife and fork and squashed some peas on to the prongs.

But Mother persisted. 'An interesting young man, Dora? Now who could that be? Did you converse with Major Bentham's son after chapel? No, you were with me, I don't think we were talking with the Benthams.'

Father interrupted, 'John Bentham's boy is not with the Yorks. and Lancs., Winifred. He joined the. . . .'

Dora did not hear. They do not know, she thought. But she was on course now. She sailed on. 'No, it was Alfred Bosanquet, the son of the rector of St Dunstan's. His brother Humphrey is. . . .'

Father swallowed a mouthful hurriedly. 'And how, Dora, did you come to meet this young man, this son of the Reverend Bosanquet?'

'Oh, quite by chance, but he was very worried about his brother because he said there were rumours of a big push.' Dora was beginning to panic. She had not eaten any of her cheese pudding.

'There are many rumours, Dora,' said Father in dark tones, 'and many families who are concerned for the safety of their loved ones in the field. I would question the wisdom of discussing these matters with those who are not within the circle of our social and chapel acquaintances.'

'Reverend Bosanquet is a tribunal member, just as you are, Father.'

'Do not answer me back, Dora!'

It was there now, that look. Dora stared at him, willing herself not to be intimidated by it. 'Father, he is Christian, and he supports the war. What else is required of him?'

'Dora!' said her mother, shocked. 'How can you speak to your father like that?'

'Leave this to me, please, Winifred. Dora, will you explain how you are so well acquainted with the Reverend Bosanquet?'

I will not tell him, she thought. I will not be required to account for my every movement. 'You were angry with Mr Lofthouse even though he is Chapel, because he is against the war. You are angry with Mr Bosanquet because he is a rector, even though he is *for* the war. Are we to be cut off from all society, Father, because their opinions differ from our own?'

Despite the intensity of her father's look and the inner tremor it provoked in her, she felt overwhelmingly the surge of indignant confidence which she had experienced in the church after Mr Bosanquet had interrupted her joyful singing.

'Dora, go to your room.'

'Father, please do not dismiss me. I would like an answer to my question. Can we associate with those whose opinions are opposed to ours? Or must each take up the position of a martyr, as Richard did, to win your respect?'

'Dora!' Mother burst into tears. 'Oh, Arnold! They're all turning against us. First Richard, then Edwin, now Dora!'

Father's hands were trembling, and that weariness which had begun with Richard and the gout was now written all over him. 'Look what you have done, Dora. Look at your mother. Do you not think she and I have had enough . . . enough pain and anxiety for one year without open rebellion from you? You will go to your room immediately. You will pray for a sense of shame, and at a later date you will ask your mother's forgiveness. Take your plate of food to the kitchen, and go.'

Dora felt the old mixture of remorse and fury creeping over her, but she was determined not to let it end there. She stood up. 'I will go to my room, Father, but I wish to tell you one or two things first. Please don't cry, Mother. I hate to upset you, I honestly do. But Father, you must let me have some opinions of my own. You have always taught me what to think, you have given me a good education and I am grateful for it, but now I am sixteen and I must think about my own life, just as Richard did. He could see his way clearly, there was an issue which he could make a stand on. But I don't have an issue like that. I am a girl – a woman – and I can't be dependent on men, because the men that girls like me might have married are being killed every day in France. I've got to have ideas of my own . . . I've got to talk about things with Phoebe and Miss Gossage and even people like Mr Bosanquet.'

'Arnold,' said Mother, blowing her nose, 'she's upset, it's all because of her age. . . .'

'It's not that, Mother. Well, that's only part of it.' She could hardly see Father's face; there were tears in her eyes. 'I'm growing up, Father, and I want to have friends of my own and ideas of my own and even think about what's going to happen to me when I leave Miss Gossage's, whether I might even be clever enough to go on, well somewhere else. . . . I don't want to be *wasted,* I . . . I'm going to my room now. Good night.'

Lizzie came out of the kitchen and saw her as she ran upstairs. As she flopped on to her bed, Lizzie followed her into the room.

'Oh Lizzie, Lizzie!'

'There, Miss Dora, there.'

Dora clung to Lizzie's ample bosom and wept.

Nineteen

IT WAS QUITE extraordinary. Nothing more was said. Breakfast on Sunday was eaten in silence, chapel followed, Father went out for an afternoon walk, chapel again, and Dora went early to bed without being told. Monday came, and she went to Miss Gossage's as usual. Monday evening passed with conversation only about the difficulty of keeping the Shop adequately stocked these days and Lizzie's astringent comments on Fanny's departure. Dora knew that there was to be no retribution. She had won.

Today, she thought on Tuesday, I will ask Miss Gossage about those examinations. She would want to tell Phoebe about it straightaway, so she asked her mother before setting off for school whether she could go straight to the manse in the afternoon. Her mother agreed.

She was a minute or two late for school, and as she took her place at her desk she noticed a very unusual thing. Miss Gossage was sitting at her desk as she always did, but she was reading a newspaper. The girls shuffled and whispered, and then sat still and gazed at her in expectation.

'Well, girls,' Miss Gossage said after a few moments, 'it has happened at last. They have made their offensive on the Somme.'

There was a rustle among the girls. Some looked blank, some puzzled, some anxious.

'Will it end the war, then, Miss Gossage, and will everything be ordinary again?' asked Minnie Chapman.

'That I cannot tell you,' replied Miss Gossage. 'Certainly General Haig hopes that it will bring the war to a swift conclusion. I do find it difficult to interpret newspaper reports.' She sounded less than her usual confident self. 'Listen to this, from *The Times*. "Sir Douglas Haig telephoned last night, that the situation was favourable." I would say that the language there is moderate in the extreme. "Effective progress," he goes on and then ". . . substantial progress . . . there is a fair field and no favour, and we have elected to fight out our quarrel with the Germans and give them as much battle as they want." ' She seemed to sink into her own thoughts. 'That is not good. It is not good at all.'

Dora was bursting with questions but could not bear to ask them in front of all the other girls. Miss Gossage turned unenthusiastically to Milton's *Comus,* but soon tired of it and suggested they return to their patchwork.

'Dora,' she said as Dora approached with her sewing, 'you look pale. Have you been having another of your fainting attacks? Or is there news of Richard?'

'I have discovered that, er, the fainting is due to, well, natural causes, Miss Gossage. No, I am afraid that we have no further news of Richard, though Mr Lofthouse says he is on to a trail which might lead somewhere. I think this piece of blue might divide into four, would it, Miss Gossage? Miss Gossage . . . ?'

'Yes, Dora? Take what you need, Mabel, and sit down. Dora?'

'This, well, battle on the Somme.' It was strange; she could face up to Father but felt shaky talking to Miss Gossage. 'Have you any idea which regiments are involved?'

'I have no idea at all, I'm afraid, Dora. As you know, I do not pursue that aspect of the war very closely. But it is clear that a large proportion of our forces must be fighting.'

'Oh. I see.'

'Are you concerned,' Miss Gossage asked quietly, 'for

the Bosanquet boy?'

Dora thought it odd that Miss Gossage should see Humphrey as a boy. 'Yes, yes I am. His father gave me some letters which I must return.'

'Dora! You have kept some letters from before the time I asked you not to be in further contact with the family?'

Dora blushed. 'No, I went again. At Whitsuntide. That letter you brought me was from Alfred. He said he might be there.'

'I see. It intrigues me, Dora, just which member of the Bosanquet family is the main object of your attention. Well, you have some letters. You must return them. You will also wish to find out, if you can, whether the elder son is in danger, though I doubt whether they will have any more definite information than I have. Leave it a day or two, Dora. On Thursday I will tell the girls that there is a special errand you must do for me.'

That must be what she told the girls on each of the other occasions, thought Dora. She, at any rate, wants me to meet all kinds of different people and have ideas of my own.

It was not until she was on her way to Phoebe's that she remembered her intention of asking about examinations. That would have to wait, she thought. She could not concentrate on anything else until she was easy in her mind about Humphrey.

Thursday came. It was very hot, even for July, and Miss Gossage opened all the schoolroom windows. At about a quarter to eleven she beckoned Dora to the front and said something quietly in her ear. Dora went out.

She decided to leave her bicycle behind and walk to the church. She had to carry the letters, and she did not want to arrive there damp and panting. As she walked up the hill she noticed the greenness of the trees against the blueness of the sky, and wondered whether it was as hot as this in France. There would be swarms of flies on the battlefield. How did they bury the bodies, anyway?

Wounds would be festering under sweating bandages. Stretcher-bearers would faint in the heat, would drop their charges who would shriek with pain. The air in the field hospitals would be stifling, the smell of gas and rotting flesh would pervade every corner. . . .

She walked slowly up the gravel path, feeling the cool shadow of the yews. The outer church door creaked a little, the inner door hardly made a sound.

The church was bathed in sunshine. It came streaming towards her from the south windows and the great east window, bringing with it all the brilliant colours of the stained glass. She was dazzled, and closed her eyes. The colours stayed with her, subtly changed.

She opened her eyes again and stood quietly. Her eyes began to adjust to the light, and she looked around.

A black figure was slumped in a pew, only a few yards from her. She knew at once that it was the rector.

She went on standing, still as stone, staring at the pew. He might be in prayer; he might be ill; he might be dead. She stared at him, frozen. Her palms were damp and her breathing shallow. Her heart felt like a drum inside her.

Without wondering whether or not she should do so, she walked quietly forward and sat down in the pew beside him. There was a copy of *The Times* in the pew in front.

He must have heard the tap of her summer shoes and the rustle of her dress, for he shifted slightly. But for a moment longer he stayed in the same position on the seat with his head in his hands against the pew in front.

She sat there, wondering how long she should stay if he did not move from his position. She thought that perhaps she should pray. She had never been very good at praying. But the words floated through her mind: 'Our Father Which Art in Heaven. Our Father Which Art in Heaven. Our Father Which Art in Heaven.'

He moved. She hardly dared look at him, for she could feel that he was making an enormous effort. But she did turn a little and as she did so he pulled himself up, slowly.

He turned towards her, his head still bowed. She could see that he had been weeping. The Lord's Prayer left her, and she could only find the word *broken*. He was broken.

Hesitantly, she put out a hand and laid it on his arm. His shoulders heaved, and he turned towards her fully and clasped her. He was weeping now; he was trembling soundlessly. She sat awkwardly, one hand still on his arm, the other dangling down at her side, and then she thought, 'I must comfort him as I would a child.' She put her arms round him and, remembering how she had occasionally held Edwin when he had fallen in the garden, she held this man in her arms until his trembling stopped.

Eventually she said, against the side of his head, 'Have you heard?'

He drew away from her. She could feel his paralysing shame and embarrassment. He shook his head with difficulty and indicated the newspaper lying on the pew. She stared at it, and wondered whether the names of the dead could possibly be listed in *The Times* so soon after the event. No; she was sure it was not so; a telegram was always sent.

'You have had no telegram? Then he may be safe. You must not fear the worst.'

He clasped his hands together and bowed his head. 'My wife. She has premonitions.' She realized that these were the first words he had spoken. 'She knows that he is dead.'

Strange visions came to Dora of Mrs Bosanquet as a medium communicating in a shadowy back-room at the rectory with a Humphrey who was beyond the grave. 'How is your wife?'

He shook his head, as if there were no words for his wife's condition.

'Will Alfred be coming home soon?'

Again he shook his head. Either he did not know, or he did not care.

Suddenly he got up, said 'Excuse me,' and quickly walked along the pew, up the side aisle and into the vestry. She watched him go. Had he left the church? Should she go, or wait for him here?

But he had left the vestry door open, and she did not hear the bang of another door, only a few rustling sounds. It seemed an hour before he returned, but it could only have been a few minutes. He walked steadily down the centre aisle. He had straightened his hair and recovered his dignity. The child had gone, the rector had returned.

But his voice was low and strained. 'You have come to return the letters?' He remained standing in the aisle beside her.

'Yes.'

She picked up the small package which she had put down on the pew and handed it to him. He picked up *The Times*, put Humphrey's letters between the pages, and held it firmly in his hand.

'Well,' he said stiffly, 'I must return to the rectory. I have to, er, prepare a sermon.'

She stood up, and he stepped aside so that she could walk out in front of him. At each of the church doors he leaned forward and pulled the door open for her.

Outside in the brilliant sunshine he put out his hand to her formally.

'Good-day, Miss Fishwick.' He clasped her hand tighter, until it almost hurt. 'Thank you . . . thank you for your sympathy.' He cleared his throat, dropped her hand, and turned abruptly to walk across to the rectory.

She felt totally disinclined to return to the classroom. She was absorbed in the rector and his family to the exclusion of everything else. There was no part of her that relished the excitement and drama and tragedy: she only felt the great weight of the anguish she had come face to face with. She walked a few paces along the path and then stood, not knowing what to do or where to go. She could perhaps go back into the church. Or she could walk over to the Green and lie down on the dry grass or sit in the shade of the trees at the foot of the Green. She stood, wavering in indecision, shivering in the sunshine between the yews.

'Miss Fishwick!'

There were footsteps crushing the gravel.

She turned around. The rector was running, his black cassock emphasizing the awkwardness of his movements as he ran.

She thought instantly, seeing his face, the telegram has arrived. She ran back, turned by the church door and ran along the path towards him.

He stopped before she did. She could see that he was shaking, not trembling but shaking.

'Mr. . . .' She was still uncertain how to pronounce it. 'What is it?'

He opened his mouth, but closed it again. She could find no words, then or later, for the look on his face. It was so unmistakably a look of death that she hardly dared ask more. But she said again, 'What is it?'

He shook his head. She thought he wanted to run, but could not think where to run to.

'A telegram?'

Again he shook his head. He put his hands over his face. Perhaps, she thought, he is going to faint.

'I will come back with you to the house.'

'No . . . no!'

'But why not? You must sit down . . . rest. . . .'

'No! No! She is. . . .'

'She?'

'Mrs Bosanquet.'

Now she heard footsteps on the gravel behind her, but the sound only registered in a small corner of her mind.

'Mrs Bosanquet?' she repeated.

He looked over her shoulder at the person who had come up the path. It was as if he could say the words to a stranger, but not to her. 'She is in the kitchen. A rope . . . she . . . a chair . . . over . . . she has hanged herself.'

Then Phoebe spoke, and the only coherent thought in Dora's head was, 'She did not hear. Phoebe did not hear what Mr Bosanquet said.'

'Dora, where on earth have you been?' said Phoebe,

irritable and breathless, and then, 'Oh, excuse me, sir, but I've been running all over the place for her. Your mother said you *must* be at Miss Gossage's. Well, I'd been there already and Miss Gossage said you'd gone. Anyway I went back and eventually she told me that I might find you near St Dunstan's! Well, here you are at last and you must come home, *my* mother's there talking to *your* mother because there's news at last of Richard.'

Twenty

MISS GOSSAGE came to see Dora just as she had done on the last occasion Dora was in bed, and again brought a letter. But this letter was from all the girls; it was covered in scribbled messages and signatures and exclamation marks and little posies of flowers painted by Minnie Chapman.

'I told them a little of what had happened,' said Miss Gossage. 'Betsy burst into tears and Minnie was unduly eager for more details. I have come with all their good wishes, and my own, too. How are you, Dora?'

Dora had assumed that there were no more tears left in her to weep, for she had wept and wept yesterday, all over Mother and over Phoebe and over Mrs Lofthouse and even a little over Father in the evening. Father had held her hand, which she could not remember his ever having done before, and said, 'Dora, Dora.' Now, with Miss Gossage, the tears started again. Miss Gossage lent her a handkerchief just as when she had wept in the classroom.

'How is Phoebe?'

'Rather weepy, I'm afraid, like me.'

'You were both very brave. You especially, Dora. Many girls would have fled or fainted. It was providential that Phoebe was there and could run for Dr Fuller. But it was you who went back to the rectory with Mr Bosanquet.'

'How is he, Miss Gossage? Do you know?'

'His sister has come from Wakefield, I hear, and Alfred is to return home tomorrow.' Miss Gossage looked at Dora, her eyes narrowing. 'Dora, have you ever before seen a person who is dead?'

'Only Grandmother Fishwick when I was four. She was in bed . . . her eyes were closed.'

'Dora, dear. It must have been a severe shock to you. Did you sleep last night?'

Tears welled up again. 'Dr Fuller gave me a sleeping-draught. It gave me a headache this morning. Miss Gossage, I keep seeing her. . . .'

'Yes, Dora, I expect you do. But it will be easier next time you have to face something like that. Yes, let us be realistic, there will be a next time. Think how much stronger and more experienced you will be then. Now. . . .' She got up, took the girls' letter and propped it up on the mantlepiece and sat down again '. . . Wipe your eyes and tell me about Richard.'

Dora wiped her eyes. It took her a few minutes to find her voice again, but eventually she said, 'He is in Armley Prison, Miss Gossage. Armley! We went to a special chapel service once in Leeds and I caught a glimpse of it, it's like a fortress. He's been there since the end of May. As soon as Mr Lofthouse had news of him, that was yesterday morning – he had a letter from the No-Conscription people, I think you know what I mean. . . .'

'The No-Conscription Fellowship.'

'Yes. Well, he had the letter at eight o'clock and took the train straight away to Leeds. He went to the prison and saw Richard and then sent a telegram to Mrs Lofthouse. What a telegram, Miss Gossage! Phoebe gave it to me, I've got it here somewhere – yes, here. RICHARD PALE AND THIN STOP HAS BEEN A THIRD DIVISION PRISONER BECAUSE OF ABSOLUTISM STOP HAVE DISCUSSED NON-ABSOLUTISM WITH HIM STOP HE WILL CONSIDER IT STOP PLEASE GIVE NEWS AND HIS GREETINGS TO HIS FAMILY STOP WILL RETURN IMMEDIATELY STOP RAYMOND. Phoebe explained what it means. I suppose you know what "absolutism" and "third division prisoners" are, Miss Gossage?'

Miss Gossage nodded and smiled gravely. 'I expect he

has made everyone at Armley very angry. Refusing to speak to warders, or persistently speaking to other prisoners, refusing to work, refusing. . . . I hope he has not been refusing to eat or sleep.'

'It says, "pale and thin".'

'He would be more than pale and thin if he had been on hunger strike, Dora. I wonder what has driven him to this course of action? Did he perhaps see his transfer to civil prison as some kind of, well, appeasement, perhaps?' She was talking to herself rather than to Dora. Then she asked, briskly, 'Well, and when Mr Lofthouse returned, did he have any more detailed news?'

'He spent a long time in the drawing-room with Father and Mother, but then Lizzie came to give me Dr Fuller's sleeping-draught and this morning Mother just said I must rest and not worry about Richard. You know that Phoebe and I thought he might have been sent to France, Miss Gossage?'

'Yes. Those men have been sentenced to life imprisonment.'

'I know. Richard has only got two years to serve.' She shivered under her blankets. 'Two years, Miss Gossage! I shall be eighteen!'

Miss Gossage got up. 'Well, Dora, that brings me to something I want to discuss with you. But it must wait until our minds are clear. Now, I am going to the rectory to see if there is anything I can do. It will be a difficult and painful time.' She paused, and then leaned towards Dora and said quietly, 'Dora, I must tell you that Dr Fuller has, in the name of charity, signed his name to a falsehood. He has said that Mrs Bosanquet was trying to take some ham off the hook when she became entangled in the rope, and fell.'

Dora did not know what to say. She began to shiver again. 'How . . . how did you know what really happened?'

'I guessed,' said Miss Gossage. 'In fact, many people will make the same guess, though they will say nothing.'

She went on, 'You are the only person, other than the rector, who will ever be certain of it, Dora. Except perhaps Phoebe? You think not. And, of course, you will tell no one.' It was put as a fact, not given as an order. 'You realize why Dr Fuller has had to do this?'

Dora nodded.

'He did it, as I say, out of charity, out of humanity. Such an unhappy woman should not be condemned as a criminal. I think you want to weep again, Dora. There is no need to be ashamed of it. I will ask your mother to bring you up a drink in a quarter of an hour's time.'

She left, and Dora buried her face in the pillow.

How extraordinary, Dora thought fleetingly as she took in the cream-white and the gold and the red, to be shaking hands with a bishop. The bishop's hand was soft and podgy and held hers only briefly and limply. She glanced up at his face: he had a fixed but not unpleasant smile. It was even more extraordinary to wait for Mother and Father as they shook hands with the bishop, too.

So many people were there. In fact, almost everybody she knew was there, and many, many more whom she did not know. The Lofthouses, the Chapmans, the Fullers, even the chapel Harmers (Mr and Mrs Harmer greeted them, and Frederick looked embarrassed), the lean chairman of the tribunal with a large tight-corseted wife, the red-faced railway clerk – Dora tired of looking at people, for many of them looked curiously at her, and she turned her eyes down at her black coat, black stockings and black boots (so hot, she was, in boots, but Father had insisted on them; she thought of the cool, cool stone against her stockinged feet on that remote day so many million years ago). People shook hands, smiled, greeted each other. With just a little more laughter it could have been a congregation social rather than a funeral.

But Reverend Bosanquet looked a ghostly grey. Alfred stuck to his side, his lip trembling and his eyes red-rimmed. There was a circle of quiet around them as they stood outside the church. It was a bright day with a high wind: the yew trees creaked and people had to hold on to their black hats.

When they turned away from the bishop, the Fishwicks walked away from the church and stood awkwardly. This was unfamiliar territory, and they did not know how to behave. Dora looked at peoples' shadows and black shoes on the gravel path and on the grass. Then she looked up and saw that Mr Bosanquet was talking to a small buxom woman who wore dark purple flowers in her black hat. They spoke a few words and then looked over in her direction.

The small buxom woman walked over. 'Miss Fishwick, Mr and Mrs Fishwick, the family and a few close friends are coming back with us to the rectory. I wonder, would you care to join us?'

Dora looked immediately at Father, and found that he had momentarily lost control of his facial expression. He was astounded. Then he looked briefly at Dora, at his wife and then turned abruptly back to the rector's sister. 'Thank you, Mrs. . . .'

'Miss Bosanquet.'

'Miss Bosanquet. That is most kind.'

On the way along the path, passing the spot where she and Phoebe and the rector had stood less than a week ago, Dora's mother leaned towards her and murmured, 'This will not distress you too much, dear?'

Dora shook her head, but said quietly, 'Will you stay by me, Mother?'

They did not, of course, go into the kitchen. The rectory drawing-room was large and airy, and two maids came silently in and out with cucumber sandwiches and iced biscuits. The bishop was there and spent some time talking to Miss Bosanquet. Mr Bosanquet moved around nodding and speaking to each person as a bridegroom would at a wedding, but he never smiled.

Father and Mother and Dora stayed together, Father

standing and talking either to no one or to the tribunal chairman who turned out to be a cousin of the Bosanquets, and Mother and Dora sitting quietly together on a small chintz settee. Dora had just refused a cucumber sandwich for the third time when Alfred came over.

'Miss Fishwick, oh, Miss Fishwick.'

Dora looked at him and felt sorry for him. For a moment she wished she could like him enough to comfort him as he needed. 'Mother, may I introduce Mr Alfred Bosanquet? My mother, Mrs Fishwick.'

Alfred shook hands gravely with Mrs Fishwick and then said, 'Miss Fishwick, I cannot thank you enough . . . for your kindness, your courage. . . .'

'You are very kind, Mr Bosanquet,' Dora's mother interrupted him. 'May we give you our deepest sympathies? What a terrible shock. . . .'

'But Miss Fishwick. . . .' Dora was amazed at his breaking into Mother's condolences, but he went on, 'I must tell you – excuse me, Mrs Fishwick – but we have had a telegram. Humphrey is wounded. In the leg and the hip. It is what they call a Blighty one. He is coming home.'

At this point Alfred's aunt retrieved him to speak to some distant relations. For a few moments Dora felt cocooned in quietness, as if all the other people in the sunny rectory drawing-room were moving behind a transparent silk screen and she was alone. She felt only the presence of Mrs Bosanquet, who must have sat silently on this settee for so many hours and days and months, longing for Humphrey's return and growing more and more certain that he would never, never come.

'Dora.' Father had been talking to Mr Bosanquet, and now put his hand on her shoulder.

Mother said quickly, 'Arnold, I think perhaps we should go home shortly. Dora is looking extremely pale.'

'Of course, Winifred. But the rector has just told me that his elder son is wounded and is soon to be brought home. I have told him our news of Richard also.'

Mother stood up, and Dora after her. 'I am so glad, Mr Bosanquet,' she said warmly. 'We can neither of us perhaps rejoice, but there is a sense in which we can all. . . .' She ran out of words.

'I understand, Mrs Fishwick,' said the rector in his deep, strained voice. 'Perhaps, if you are able to visit your son, Fishwick, you would give him my sincerest good wishes.' He looked very ill at ease, and Dora thought he was going to turn away. But he did not: he suddenly stared at her and went on staring for several moments, before saying in his old sharp bark, 'My thanks are due to you, Miss Fishwick. And my profound distress that you should have had to. . . .' He stopped, and spoke abruptly to Father. 'You have reason to be proud of your daughter, Fishwick. She has qualities which I would prize in a daughter of my own. Do not . . . do not let them be wasted.'

Father, surprised, said, 'Indeed I will not.'

They said their goodbyes, quickly, and left.

Twenty-one

'RICHARD, RICHARD, Richard!' shouted Edwin as Father came up the path. 'Where's Richard, Richard?'

'No, no, Edwin dear, Richard isn't. . . .'

'He is in Leeds, Edwin,' said Father firmly, coming in and taking off his hat. 'He sends his love to you all – to you as well, Lizzie. Now, if Lizzie will kindly take Edwin to have his tea, perhaps I could rest in the drawing-room after my journey – yes, Dora, do not look so impatient – and then I will tell you all about it.'

When Father had removed his coat and been upstairs and come down again and settled himself at last in his chair with the footstool, Dora and her mother leaned forward and waited for him to speak.

He smiled. 'As I said, Richard sends his love to you all. He told me that it was the thought of your – our – affection for him, together with Mr Lofthouse's prayerful support, that has sustained him during these difficult months.'

'Arnold, is he very thin? I cannot bear to think of him wasting away.'

'He is certainly very spare, Winifred, but then he never was what one would call sturdy. In fact his period of, well, resistance lasted only a matter of weeks, and during that time he refused to eat for only a few days.'

'But, Arnold, *why* should he refuse to *eat*?'

'Well, I think we must try to understand that Richard has been making a stand against a system which assumes that men who refuse to be soldiers must have all rights taken away from them.' It was strange to hear Father lecturing to them on such a subject. 'While he was in military detention, the routine was extremely harsh – no mattress to sleep on, work in all waking hours, little recreation and frequent punishments.' Dora saw Mother shudder. 'Strangely enough, this was a regime that Richard could accept. It was what he had expected, and though it was hard there were others of like mind who were enduring it with him, and he could tolerate it.'

'But why did he not *write* to us, Father?'

'He did, Dora. But his letters never reached us. He assumes that they were considered unsuitable and were confiscated by the censor.'

'Oh.'

'But then he was transferred to Armley.'

'Was that not a relief to him, Arnold, to be in civilian custody and no longer expected to do military drill?'

'I think, Winifred, that it is at this point that we must make the most difficult adjustment to our customary thinking.' He shifted his foot to a more comfortable position on its stool. 'Richard tells me that he felt defeated. In civil prison, he could no longer make a stand against the war and what he calls the "military machine". There were many conscientious objectors who did find it a relief, as you say. But a few, of whom Richard was one, decided to take an "absolutist" stand. They wanted to show that they were not ordinary civil criminals and were still unflinching in their adherence to the cause of peace. So they flouted the prison rules in every way they could. If they should speak, they did not. If they should keep silence, they spoke. If they should work, they refused. They refused food, some of them even refused to sleep. And many are continuing to take this stand.'

Mother closed her eyes and then opened them again. 'And Richard – will he continue like this?'

'No, my dear. Mr Lofthouse has persuaded him against it. Winifred, we have been unjust to Mr Lofthouse. We have greatly underestimated his courage and wisdom. Richard told me that far from encouraging him in his martyr-like stance Mr Lofthouse made one or two remarks to him which could almost be construed as cruel.'

'Cruel?' Dora could not believe it.

'He pointed out to Richard that a martyr sometimes seeks his own destruction in order to hurt those who have, in good conscience, disagreed with him.' Mother looked up at him. 'I understand by that, Winifred, that Richard was making a stand not only against war, but against his family. Against myself.' Father turned and stared out of the window.

'I cannot understand it . . . I cannot believe it, Arnold.'

'I cannot fully understand it myself, Winifred. Perhaps Dora is in a better position to understand than we are.'

Mother looked at Dora, puzzled, and then got up. 'I must see to Edwin. Well, Richard is a different boy from the one I imagined him to be. I remember him when he was Edwin's age – he was so docile.'

Father seemed to have a glint in his eye as Mother closed the door behind her. 'One thing that can be said about you, Dora, is that you have never been *docile*.'

'Not even as an infant, Father?'

'How good to see you smile, Dora. I hoped that this tragedy and the conflicts that have beset us recently had not banished your smile for ever.'

'I have had the same thought about you, Father.'

They were silent for a few moments, and Dora was unwilling to break the silence.

Father said quietly, 'You may be aware, Dora, that until recently Richard was something of a disappointment to me. I had great hopes for him – no, not in the Shop. I did not want him to take over the Shop. I saw him as a great preacher or missionary, a Booth, perhaps, or a Livingstone. It was the path I would have chosen for myself, had your uncle Richard not been killed, leaving the Shop with no-one but myself to take it over from your grandfather.'

Dora was tempted to go over and kneel on the floor beside Father's chair, but she could not bring herself to do so.

'What Richard's future is now,' he went on, 'who can tell? I have no doubt that he will be in prison for the duration of the war, and no one knows how long that will be. Have you seen the casualty lists in the *Post* during the last week?' Dora nodded. 'It is terrible . . . terrible. There is something in me which thanks God that Richard is not there. But Dora, it occurred to me as I travelled back in the train from Leeds this afternoon, that there is someone else's future which is also worth consideration. Miss Gossage has been to see me. . . .'

Dora was startled.

'Yes, you are not the only one with secrets, Dora. Miss Gossage made some suggestions about your prospects which are not entirely repugnant to me.'

Her mind went blank. She could hardly think what Miss Gossage's suggestions had been.

'She holds your intelligence in high regard, Dora. She tells me that you not only have natural aptitudes, but that you also possess diligence and application. It is her wish that you should take the examinations that would enable you to pursue your education at college or university.'

'Father! I wanted . . . I hoped . . . but is your opinion not that it is a waste to educate a girl, when her only prospect is the care of a home and family?'

'It may or may not be so. But what could be more of a waste than letting the money I have set aside for Richard's education lie idle while he is . . . while he is being taken care of elsewhere?'

'Edwin?'

'There is time enough to think of Edwin, Dora. At the moment I prefer to think of you. Now, I have been frank with you: perhaps you will have the kindness to be frank with me. Could you tell me all that has happened in recent weeks that you think I would wish to know?'

Mrs Lofthouse strode ahead of them along Banderbridge Road, in the company of an acquaintance who was taking a basket of fruit to the hospital.

'Do you think you'll faint, Dora?' asked Phoebe. 'You know what you're like.'

'I don't faint at times like *that*, Phoebe. I didn't faint. . . .' She was going to say 'when I saw Mrs Bosanquet', but she could not bring the words out. She was angry with herself. 'I'll be just as good at it as you are, you'll see. So long as your mother will show me what to do.'

'Of course she will, or one of the other nurses. We'll be ever so busy, you won't be able to hover all the time like the Lady with the Lamp at Humphrey Bosanquet's bedside, you know.'

'You don't have to tell me that. I'll take no more notice of him than I do of the other patients.'

Phoebe grinned. 'I expect Mother would be shocked at your hard-heartedness if you didn't go over and hold his hand for a moment and give him your sympathies.'

'Oh, shut up, Phoebe.' Dora was extremely nervous, and half-wished she could run back home.

'Look at old Mrs Bunn with her fruit,' said Phoebe. 'It's almost as broad as she is. How does she manage to balance that weight on those spindly legs? Dora, how's your diary going?'

She shook her head. 'I've written nothing. Nil, zero, blank page. Not for weeks.'

'Not about . . . ?'

'Not about *anything*. There's too much to say.'

'Too *much*?'

'And no words.'

'Well, you are funny, Dora. I'll never understand you. And I wanted to read it. I was going to let you read mine, but I'm not sure that I will now.'

'Oh, go on, Phoebe, what does it say? That you're lovesick for Richard?'

'Wouldn't you like to know? Maybe I'm set on your Humphrey!'

'You aren't! Oh Phoebe, don't tease.'

'I'm sorry, Dora. You are still a bit, well, shaky, aren't you? Don't worry, I won't take Humphrey away from you.'

'He isn't even mine!'

'I know, I know. Look, there's the hospital, we'd better not quarrel. I'll tell you about all the things you've got to do. Rule number one: you must never let a single *strand* of your hair out from under your cap. Rule number two: you must call all the officers sir, and that includes Humphrey. Rule number three. . . .'

Dora hardly listened. She knew that Mrs Lofthouse would tell her all of it again at least three times when they got there. She tried to picture Humphrey lying wounded in the hospital bed, and found it impossible. She tried to picture herself as an assistant nurse, and that was even more impossible. She could half-see herself as a student with a black gown rather like Mr Bosanquet's cassock flowing out behind her, but even that image was a blurred one. She could only be sure of her own firm tread on the cinder path, of the steps of the makeshift hospital rising before her, and her own voice saying, 'Yes, Mrs Lofthouse, it would be good if I could see him first. Which direction do I take?'

When Hitler Stole Pink Rabbit

Judith Kerr

Anna was only nine in 1933, too busy with her school work and her friends to take much notice of the posters of Adolf Hitler and the menacing swastikas plastered over Berlin. Being Jewish, she thought, was just something you were because your parents and grandparents were Jewish.

Suddenly, Anna's father was unaccountably missing. Shortly after, she and her brother were hurried out of Germany by their mother with alarming secrecy. Then began their rootless, wandering existence as refugees. Their life was often difficult and sad, but Anna soon discovered that all that really mattered was that the family was together.

An outstanding book for readers of ten upwards.